The Las

Book Two

Lone Star Joy

The Lasso Spring Series

Book Two

Lone Star Joy

By

Kathleen Ball

The Lasso Springs Series

Book One: Callie's Heart
Book Two: Lone Star Joy
Book Three: Stetson's Storm

Desert Breeze Publishing, Inc.
27305 W. Live Oak Rd #424
Castaic, CA 91384

http://www.DesertBreezePublishing.com

Copyright © 2012 by Kathleen Ball
ISBN 10: 1-61252-853-8
ISBN 13: 978-1-61252-853-3

Published in the United States of America
Electronic Publish Date: September 2012
Print Publish Date: August 2013

Editor-In-Chief: Gail R. Delaney
Content Editor: Sarah Giese
Marketing Director: Jenifer Ranieri
Cover Artist: Gwen Phifer

Cover Art Copyright by Desert Breeze Publishing, Inc © 2012

All rights reserved. No portion of this book may be reproduced or transmitted in any form or by any electronic or mechanical means, including photocopying, recording or by any information retrieval and storage system without permission of the publisher.

Names, characters and incidents depicted in this book are products of the author's imagination, or are used in a fictitious situation. Any resemblances to actual events, locations, organizations, incidents or persons – living or dead – are coincidental and beyond the intent of the author.

Dedication

I dedicate *Lone Star Joy* to my wonderful in-laws, Jinny and Charlie Ball, for all of their support through the years.

I also dedicate *Lone Star Joy* to my friend Jeannie Steven for always being there for me.

Thank you to Sarah Giese, my editor for *Lone Star Joy,* and Theresa Stillwagon, my editor for *Callie's Heart.*

A very special thank you to Desert Breeze Publishing, for taking a chance on me.

And of course I dedicate *Lone Star Joy* to my three guys -- Bruce, Steven, and Colt -- because I love them.

Chapter One

Joy Courtland glanced down at the address on the ragged piece of paper she held in her shaking hand and compared it to the number on the house, confirming that she'd found the right place. She had expected someone to meet her at the bus station. In fact, her parole officer had insisted on it. Luckily she'd found a ride.

Standing in front of the heavy wooden door, the century-old log house loomed large. The two-story farmhouse with its black shutters and wraparound porch looked enormous and intimidating. Joy hoped that she could just do her work release program and be left alone. She wasn't there to make friends; she was there to be free. The idea of freedom made her almost smile.

Before Joy had a chance to knock, the door swung open. A tall, frazzled man with jet-black hair and dark eyes stood holding a crying baby. Before she could even open her mouth, the man shoved the baby into her arms and yelled something about being back in a few.

Joy looked down at the howling little baby in her arms and frowned. Figuring that Mr. Walker must have an emergency to attend to, she walked into the kitchen, found a bottle, and warmed it. She sat in the comfy rocking chair in the family room and fed the little one.

Blissful silence filled the house. "You sure have big lungs. Inherited them from your daddy did you?"

Joy wanted to smile, but it wasn't something she readily did. The baby finished its bottle and Joy burped it.

"Let's go get you changed and then I'll know which it is you are." She stood up and carried the baby upstairs. Finding the baby's room was easy enough. The blue walls were a bit faded, but the cowboy border looked new. Perhaps a boy, but she would have liked cowboys in her room when she was young. The crib and matching changing table looked new. "Well what do you know, a little boy," she exclaimed, as she changed his diaper. Joy tried to lay him in his crib, but he just howled at her, so she held him and went back downstairs to the rocking chair.

There was a phone next to the chair. Her first priority was to call George, her parole officer. He'd gone out of his way to get this work release for her and she wasn't going to pay him back by breaking the rules.

"Hello?"

"George, it's me, Joy. I'm at the Walker spread and calling as instructed." Her voice quavered. It had been a long time since she'd used a phone.

"Good, glad to hear it. Put Mr. Walker on the phone."

"He's not here. He handed me a baby and ran out the door."

George laughed. "Well I know you're at the right place. You all right with the baby?"

"I used to babysit once in a while before -- well before."

"It's fine, Joy. Look forward, not back. Just have Mr. Walker call me when he gets back."

"I will, and, George? Thank you."

She leaned back in the rocking chair and relaxed more than she had in more than eight years. Finally, her eyes closed.

*****

Stamos stood over his new housekeeper and frowned. She looked a bit young to him. Hell, if she could get Dillon to sleep every night it would be worth it. He touched her shoulder. The panic in her big hazel eyes surprised him. "It's just me," he assured her.

Joy blinked twice and looked around the room. "What?"

"You must have fallen asleep."

"Oh. Well I want you to know that I never fall asleep in the saddle."

"Honey, as long as you can keep us happy you won't have to worry about the saddle." He knew instantly that he must have said the wrong thing. Her pale face turned bright red.

"George never said. I don't do that. I..." She bit her bottom lip.

"Whoa. What's this about George?"

"He said you were on the up and up with your work release program. He never mentioned me making anyone happy."

"I think we're talking about two different things. Here give me Dillon." Stamos leaned down and took the sleeping baby from her. "Now let's start from the beginning. I'm Stamos Walker and you are?"

Her whole body tensed. "I'm Joy Courtland. I'm the horse wrangler. I'm on the prison work release program."

Stamos softly swore. "George sent you here? You're not the new housekeeper?"

Joy shook her head. "Is there a problem?"

"I don't hire women to work on my ranch. George knows it too."

"If you would just give me a chance." Her bright blue eyes were too big for her thin face. In fact, all of her looked down right thin, except for the glorious chestnut braid that hung down her back. It looked as thick as his wrist.

"Listen, can you hold Dillon while I make a phone call?"

Joy stretched out her arms and took the baby, cuddling him to her. Stamos gave her a curt nod and walked to the phone across the room.

"Well, Dillon, I guess it's back to the women's penitentiary." She looked down at Dillon and sighed. "You sure are a cute one, but I guess it makes no never mind to me." Her braid hung over her shoulder and

Dillon grabbed it. "Ouch. You little dickens. Give me my hair back." Dillon held on tighter with both hands this time.

"Well if you don't beat all. You are a handful. Full of piss and vinegar I'd say. Cute as a doodle bug, but a handful." She smiled, as she tried to pry his hands from her hair.

Stamos watched, trying not to laugh. Dillon had pulled his hair a time or two and he knew how much it hurt. This little gal acted like it was all a game. She was good with his son.

He picked up a plastic horse that was Dillon's favorite and tried to entice him with it. "Dill, come on now, let go of the sweet lady's hair."

"Dillon," Joy cajoled, "come play horsey with your daddy." She stared at Stamos. "Maybe if you made horse sounds."

Stamos thought she was a bit daft, but he tried it. Dillon immediately let go of Joy's hair, which she put behind her, and reached for the horse. "I'll be damned. It worked," he said.

"I talked to George." He watched her face close and her body tense. "It doesn't make sense. I run a work release program for non-violent offenders, male non-violent offenders. You don't qualify for either. I don't know what to do with you. I feel bad, but you'll have to go back in the morning. Will I have to worry about you running off?"

Joy just shook her head. "Just show me where to lay my head for the night and I'll be gone tomorrow. I don't want any trouble, Mr. Walker."

"Stamos."

"Stamos?"

"My name. Call me Stamos. I am sorry."

"I understand. I'm grateful for the few hours that I had outside the prison. Can I ask you a question?"

"Sure."

"Where is Dillon's mama?" Joy's face grew red. "I'm sorry I shouldn't have asked."

"She stopped by a couple months ago, handed me Dillon and told me he was my son. I haven't seen her since. In fact, I heard she left town." Stamos shook his head. "Dillon's mother is a waitress I dated, named Stacey. She never even told me she was pregnant. However, I got the best of both worlds. I have a son and I don't have to put up with an unwanted wife."

"Do you mind if I go out to the barn and look at the horses? I haven't seen one in years."

"Go right ahead. It'll give me time to figure out where to put you."

*****

She walked into the cool night. The chilled air felt liberating. Joy wished she could free her heart and her bitterness as easily. The Texas night sky surrounded her. It appeared as though she could reach up and pluck a star. It wouldn't bring her luck, nothing ever did.

The barn was something to behold. She'd rather be in a barn any day. The smell of fresh and the not so fresh hay brought back good memories. It startled her since she didn't think she had any good memories.

She poked her head into each stall and she greeted each horse. Stamos sure did know his horses, these were beauties. Wistfully she patted the paint on the neck. "So handsome, yes you are."

She heard something behind her. She stopped and listened, ready to fight. Whirling around she meant to get in the first blow. Just as her fist shot out, it was caught by Stamos' massive hand.

"Take it easy. No one will hurt you here."

Quick as lightning she disengaged from him. She wasn't used to anyone touching her. Joy was about to answer him when a downed horse caught her eye.

She ignored Stamos, let herself into the red roan's stall, and knelt next to him.

Stamos rushed in after her. "Get out of the way, I need to get him on his feet."

Shrugging, Joy scurried to one corner and watched Stamos try to get the horse on its feet. "Let me."

Stamos cursed a blue streak. "Just help me. If I can't get him up, he'll die."

"I know." Joy knelt next to the horse again. This time she laid her head on its neck, talking soothingly as she stroked him.

"What the hell?"

"Shhh." She laid her head on the horse's head. "Leave the stall, please."

"Listen lady, I don't know what you think you're doing--"

"You'll find out, just give me a minute."

Stamos left the stall.

Joy could feel his hard angry eyes on her. The horse had colic and if she couldn't get him on his feet in the next few minutes, it would be too late.

Standing in front of the red roan, Joy coaxed it to stand. "Hand me the bridle."

Stamos stared at her. "I'll be damned."

"The bridle?"

Stamos handed it to her and watched as she talked to the horse.

"Stamos, open the door. The horse and I have some walking to do."

"Franklin."

"What?" she asked, leading the horse out of the barn.

"The horse's name is Franklin."

"Frankie, let's go."

"No not Frankie, Franklin."

Joy paused and looked at Stamos. He looked serious and he looked worried. "He'll be fine, but he'll need hours of walking to work the kinks out of him."

"I'll go call the vet." Stamos turned toward his house.

Joy didn't answer him. "Frankie, we'll just take it nice and slow. No reason for either of us to wear out our shoes."

*****

Stamos finally reached Doc Parker. Doc wouldn't be able to get out to the ranch until the morning at the earliest. He was tending a pregnant mare. He did tell Stamos that he was doing everything right by keeping Franklin on his feet.

Stamos looked in on Dillon. He hated to leave him for even a minute. Grabbing the baby monitor, he headed out to find Joy. What a surprise she turned out to be. He had to admire her way with horses. If not for her, Franklin would still be down in his stall. Too bad he had to send her back. Murder was a deal breaker in his book and he couldn't have her around his son.

He stepped out into the chill of the night and scanned the area until he spotted Joy. The moonlight shone on her hair making her look angelic. He knew better and he wished he didn't know. Women were not angels.

There was something about her. She had a gentle soothing way with both horses and children. Her reflex action in the barn was natural. Most convicts had that reaction and he knew better than to sneak up on them. George's recommendation of her confused him. The parole officer knew better than to send a violent prisoner to him.

He'd wait until she walked his way, he didn't want to be away from the house. Damn, why hadn't the nanny shown? As much as he loved his son, it'd been hard trying to raise him alone.

She didn't have much of a figure. She looked similar to a beanpole, no curves in sight. Stamos wished he could help her, but he couldn't. It didn't stop him from watching her walk Franklin all around the area. He could see her talking to his roan and it made him smile. She'd been good with Dillon. Nope, he wasn't going to go there, he decided.

She walked closer and Stamos was once again reminded just how young she looked. He knew that she'd been in the State Pen for eight years. That should make her twenty-six at the youngest. She sure didn't look it.

"Want me to walk him for a while?" he offered.

Joy shook her head. "Franklin and I are just fine. The opportunity to be outside at night is a treat for me."

"Why don't you walk him in a circle on the corral?"

"Franklin would get too bored going around in circles."

Stamos looked at her earnest face and it struck him that she thought it was true.

*****

"Well lookie here. It looks like I found me a genuine woman."

Joy woke startled. A big ox of a man loomed over her. She must have fallen asleep outside of Franklin's stall.

Her plan to talk her way out of the situation derailed when the big ox grabbed her arm and hauled her to her feet. "Wait."

The smile on the man's face looked sickening. She'd seen that look on the guards' faces. Kicking him in the shins, Joy tried to dart around him to no avail.

He pushed his huge body against hers and she tried to scream. Nothing came out of her mouth.

"It's all right, Benji. Let her go," Stamos said.

Joy couldn't see him around the big man, but Stamos' presence reassured her.

She could breathe again, the big ox Benji had taken a step back. This mountain of a man was named Benji? Wasn't that a name of a cute dog?

"Aw, Boss. I was just getting to know the little gal. Besides, she asked me to kiss her."

"Listen, Benji, this is Joy. She is not to be touched by you again."

Benji looked like a sad little boy. "Okay, Stamos. I'll be good." He turned toward Joy. "I'm sorry, Joy. Do you want me to kiss you?"

"Benji. What did I just say?"

"No kissin'," he answered, morosely. "Stamos, is it all right if I feed the horses now?"

"Sure, buddy, all but Franklin. His tummy hurts."

Benji gave Stamos a solemn nod. "Sorry, Miss Joy."

Realizing that there was something off with Benji, she simply nodded.

"How's Franklin this morning?" Stamos asked, looking better than any man had a right to. Joy had to be careful. She might find herself tempted to fall into the chocolate pools of his eyes.

"I fell asleep, but he's on his feet."

"How long did you walk him? I meant to come out to check on you, but Dillon kept fussing and hell, I fell asleep too."

"We walked until dawn. You have a great roan. Franklin has fine lines, and his muscle structure is outstanding. A cow horse, right?"

Stamos smiled at her. "He's the one I ride."

"What time is George picking me up?"

"Haven't heard from him yet. He has my cell number. Why don't you come to the house and get something to eat. I don't want you around the other men until I introduce you. I don't want you mistaken for a feast again."

"Don't tell me, Benji is a gentle giant."

"Usually. He must have been taken with you though."

"Is that an insult? You make it seem a near impossibility."

Stamos laughed. "No, there's nothing wrong with you."

She swallowed hard, compliments, or near compliments were a never thing for her. In fact, having a conversation was a new concept. It'd been a long eight years and misery washed over her. When Stamos' cell phone rang, she'd be going back.

She was strong. She could get through anything. She only had three more years to serve. Her heart wanted to break, but she wouldn't allow such feelings. They were too destructive. There was no place in her life for hurt feelings.

Chapter Two

Joy stepped into the warm bath. The water caressed her body. She wanted to enjoy it, but the niggling in the back of her head wouldn't permit it. She'd allowed herself a slight glimmer of hope coming to this ranch and now... Life's disappointments had a way of finding her.

Getting out, she quickly dried herself and then wrapped her breasts. Large breasts were attention getters in prison. Only a few female guards knew her secret.

She never wore make-up and she never smiled. Joy kept her mouth shut, her eyes open, and tried to be as invisible as possible. Being a plain Jane worked in her favor at times. At other times there was nothing that could be done. If someone wanted you dead, they tried their unyielding best to get the job done. The numerous scars on her body proved it.

She dressed in the clothes Stamos had given her. Most prisoners came to his ranch with only the clothes on their backs. Almost cracking a smile, Joy slipped on the men's white briefs. It didn't matter.

She braided her hair, and opened the door. George was expected at any minute. He'd been her champion for so long, she hoped that she didn't embarrass herself by crying when she set eyes on him. It wouldn't do.

Walking into the kitchen, she found Stamos making a stack of pancakes. They smelled heavenly. Dillon lay in a playpen not far from Stamos. He looked happy with himself. He rolled one way, looked surprised, and rolled the other way looking just as surprised. He laughed in delight.

Stamos' face beamed. "He just learned to roll over. Seems to be practicing."

His smile was infectious and Joy couldn't help it, she smiled back. "He is adorable."

She wanted to pick him up and hold him, but she knew that it wouldn't be allowed. Stamos didn't want a murderer touching his son. "What time is George coming to get me?"

"Should be soon," Stamos said, not turning from the stove. "Help yourself to some breakfast."

"Thanks." It smelled wonderful, but a lump formed in her throat and she didn't know if she would be able to eat.

Joy's eyes lingered on Stamos as she sat at the table. His shoulders were broad and his rear-end looked so good in his Wranglers. The muscles in his arms left her drooling. Men were betrayers she reminded herself.

Breakfast was good. To her amazement, she smiled often. Dillon's antics caused both adults to smile at each other. There was such kindness in Stamos' eyes and for a moment, Joy wished to be part of it.

The phone rang, putting an end to all wishes. It was George. Joy watched anxiously as Stamos took the phone into his office. She heard him raise his voice a couple times, but she couldn't make out what he was saying.

Her fate had been in other's hands since she was fourteen years old. Nothing had changed in eight years.

Stamos looked put out when he walked back into the kitchen. He stood, his hands fast at his hips and a huge frown on his face. "I guess you'll be here another day."

He appeared so upset that Joy apologized.

"Not your fault. Well, let me get this little cowboy ready and we'll go out to the barn. I have a heap of work waiting."

Joy's shoulders relaxed. She had another day of freedom. She would treat it as the gift it was intended. Stamos' annoyance showed, but he'd get over it, she hoped.

Happily, she washed the dishes while Stamos got Dillon ready to go outside.

It must take a long time to get a baby ready, she reasoned, as she sat at the kitchen table waiting. However, the wait was worth it. Dillon had a little cowboy hat that matched his father's gray Stetson. Both men looked wonderful.

"So what's on tap?" Joy asked.

"I want to check on Franklin and work with a few of the other horses, mainly Monroe."

Stamos carried Dillon toward the barn and Joy followed. "Well I'm anxious to meet the other horses."

Stamos stopped and looked at her. "Don't get out of my sight until I've introduced you to the other men. I don't want any problems having a damn blame female around the ranch."

Joy turned her head away and took an unsteady breath. She never fit in anywhere. "Don't worry, I won't be a bother."

The barn exhibited chaos with approximately six cowboys arguing about Franklin. They all grew mum as soon as the boss came into sight.

"What's all the ruckus?" Stamos questioned.

"Benji's telling another whopper about a lady horse whisperer," one of the ranch hands announced.

"Could be Benj is right. This here is Joy. She fixed up Franklin last night and spent most of it walking him."

The silence struck her as deafening. Joy could feel every eye on her and she knew she didn't measure up.

"Joy, this is Corny, my foreman. Then we have Rowdy, Arlo, Shep, and Kid."

Each man tipped his hat to her.

"George sent her here by mistake, but heed my warning, as long as she is here, hands off."

"Sure, Boss," Corny said. He reminded Joy of a giant refrigerator. He looked big and solid. He had blond hair and friendly hazel eyes.

"Corny, I need you and Shep to ride to the outer perimeter and start gathering any stray cattle. Kid, you go too. Rowdy, I need you to work with Bogart. He's stopping fast enough, but he needs to turn on a dime. Arlo, buddy, I'm afraid it's your turn to muck out the stalls."

Joy watched as all the men went about their jobs. All but Arlo, who looked down hearted.

"If it's okay with Stamos, I'd like to help muck out those stalls," she offered.

Arlo's brown eyes lit up. "Sure would be kind of you ma'am."

"Stamos?" Joy asked, watching his face to see if she had overstepped her bounds.

"Have at it."

"What about Dillon?" she asked.

"I have a playpen set up in here."

"Oh good." Others might consider mucking out stalls to be the worst job, but today it seemed blissful.

Stamos watched her pick up a shovel and grab a wheel barrel. Joy could feel the heat from his gaze on her.

"Da Da, Da Da, Da Da," Dillon jabbered happily.

Stamos laughed and hugged him close. "Your first word."

Dillon smiled and drooled.

Joy turned from her task and smiled at Stamos. "He's a charmer. It must feel so good to have him say your name."

Stamos stared at her. "It's amazing." He put Dillon in his playpen. "You be good. Da Da is going to check on Franklin."

Stamos opened Franklin's stall only to have the horse balk at him. He seemed highly agitated. "It's all right boy, I'm just putting you out in the fresh air."

Franklin wouldn't settle down for him and Stamos turned toward Joy, his eyebrows furrowed.

Joy walked over to Franklin's stall and talked to him. Franklin neighed at her and butted her with his head. Joy kept talking to him, stroking his neck as she talked. She had the bridle and lead rope on and led him out of his stall. "Where to?" she asked Stamos.

"The corral." Stamos followed her out of the barn shaking his head the whole way. "So he only comes to you?"

Joy latched the fence and turned toward him. "No, not at all. He's stressed that's all. You'll see, he'll be your best friend in an hour or so." She walked into the barn. There were stalls to clean.

Dillon started to cry, she picked him up and kissed his face. Dillon started chanting, "Ma Ma, Ma Ma." She never expected that. Her heart tugged and she hugged Dillon a little closer.

"Here, give me my son before he likes you better too."

Joy handed over Dillon. The unfriendly look on Stamos' face said it all. He didn't want her to touch his son. She understood, but it hurt. It was tempting to watch Stamos get Dillon settled in the playpen, but she tore her eyes away and went back to work.

Overall, it'd been a satisfying morning, mucking out the stalls and bringing the horses outside to the pasture. Stamos had some high quality horses and it stung that she wouldn't be around to help train them.

All morning she'd been on high alert, waiting for Stamos' cell phone to ring. Mercifully it had been silent, but she didn't relax. It was bound to be any minute now.

She placed fresh hay into the last stall. She put her hands on the small of her back and stretched. Turning she noticed Arlo's eyes on her giving her an appreciative look. Joy looked away and shuddered. No matter where she was, it was always the same. No matter how plain she made herself, she still got that look from both men and women. It disgusted her. At one point, she nearly took a shiv and scarred her face. Shaking hands and vanity stopped her in the end, but there had been many times since that she regretted her cowardice.

Joy looked toward the door and noticed a perky blond entering the barn. Joy envied her ability to be carefree. She looked happy and Joy wondered how it felt. The blond located Stamos and launched herself into his arms.

Joy ached for things she could never have. It was time. Why didn't the phone ring? Joy was ready to go back to prison. The outside world was too full of emotions that she wasn't equipped to handle.

The other men started to trickle into the barn. It was lunchtime. Joy went to help with each horse. She kept her eyes open and her mouth shut, her prison way.

"The Boss is calling you," Corny said.

"Oh, thanks." She'd heard him. She just needed a second to compose herself. He probably had news from George.

Her heart dropped as she walked toward the couple. The blond gave her a hostile look. Joy figured things didn't bode well for her.

"Joy, this is Bailey. She's offered to help out until my elusive nanny shows up," Stamos explained, smiling at Bailey the whole time.

Joy nodded. "Nice to meet you."

Bailey gave her a dismissive look and turned to Stamos. "Let me get Dillon and I'll make us some lunch."

Stamos' smile was too sugary sweet for Joy. "Joy, join us. I don't want you out here with the men."

Joy started to protest.

"I noticed the look Arlo gave you. I think it'd be wise for you to stick with me today."

Joy nodded, then observed Bailey's look of outrage. If it ruined the little princess's day, Joy was all for it.

"Alright if I check on Franklin first?" Joy asked.

"Sure, just come up to the house in a few."

Joy watched the trio walk toward the house. She shrugged her shoulders and she went into the corral. Franklin came charging over to her. "Feelin' better Frankie?" she asked, looking into his eyes. "Well yes I see you are." She stroked his head.

Before she knew it, all the horses surrounded her, wanting her attention. Joy glowed at the horses. She preferred horses to people. Making her way out of the circle of horses, she caught sight of the men all lined up staring at her. Joy nodded at them and turned toward the house. She didn't care what they thought, but she thought that maybe she glimpsed a bit of respect in their eyes.

Joy could hear voices as she stood outside the back door. She wasn't surprised that she was their topic of conversation. It seemed that Bailey didn't want her in the house. Stamos didn't defend her, he explained that Joy would be gone by the afternoon.

"Hi. Am I interrupting?" she asked, stepping into the kitchen.

"Not at all," Bailey replied. "We were just talking about you. I don't think a murderer should be in the house, but Stamos doesn't want to heed my warning."

Joy looked from the brazen blonde to Stamos. He looked at the floor. No help there. "I won't kill you, today."

"Stamos. Did you hear her?" Bailey demanded.

Stamos' lips twitched. It looked as though he was trying to suppress a smile. "She's kidding." He pulled a chair out from the table. "Joy, have a seat."

"She gets to sit like a queen while I toil in the kitchen?"

"Listen, Bailey, I appreciate the help, but if you're just going to complain..."

"Oh, Stamos, you know I just want what's best for you and your little boy."

Stamos gave her a wide smile. "Good. Now I'm hungry."

Lunch became awkward with the questions that Bailey shot at her. Joy wanted to strangle her and use her blond head as a mop. Bailey asked if she had a girlfriend in prison, did she belong to the skinheads and the kicker, who did she murder and how.

Joy grew hot under the collar. She ignored Bailey for the most part. However, the last questions about the murder were too much. She jumped up and walked to the door. "I'll be out in the barn."

*****

Stamos watched her leave. She remained calmer than he would

have. Bailey was a piece of work. A rude, spoiled piece of work, but beggars couldn't be choosers. She'd always been a friend to him at the diner. He needed her to take care of Dillon.

"I have a few calls to make, I'll be in my office."

Bailey gave him one of her sultry smiles. Somehow, it made him feel dirty. He sat at his desk and reached for the phone. After a few calls, he tracked down George. He'd had a heart attack and his replacement didn't know anything about the work release program or who Joy Courtland was. After finding out that George would be all right, he hung up. He'd have to hold on to Joy until George was well. He didn't trust half of the parole officers. The main reason he started his early release program was to give these men a fair shake. He couldn't send her back until he knew she would be fine.

His second call was to the nanny service. His file had been misplaced, but they promised him someone by the end of the week. Hell, it was only Tuesday.

That left him with the problem of where Joy would be sleeping tonight. He had his non-violent offenders rule for a reason. He needed to protect his son. He couldn't take a chance. He'd think of something.

It seemed to be one thing after another lately. The shock of being an instant daddy had thrown him. He knew Dillon was his. He looked just like him. It also threw him that Stacey didn't want Dillon. What kind of mother does that?

Stamos sighed, being a rancher sure had its share of headaches, but it was better than working incessantly uncover with the FBI. Here he could breathe, he could be himself. For a while he'd been afraid that he'd lost his true self. The land, the animals, and the men grounded him and made him feel whole again.

Chapter Three

Joy stared at the sparse room in dismay. Bailey had insisted that she wouldn't sleep in the same house as a murderer. Stamos wouldn't hear of Joy sleeping in the bunkhouse, which secretly made Joy glad, but now looking at the tiny room attached to the barn, she began to rethink her luck.

"It's not much," Stamos commented.

"I'm not used to much. I'll be fine."

Stamos smiled at her. "You just go with the flow."

"It's the only way to stay alive."

Stamos' smile faded. "I know. It's sad that someone as young as you has already learned such a lesson."

"I guess I was born under an unlucky star. I've learned most of what I know the hard way."

Stamos appeared uncertain to leave.

Joy didn't want trouble. "I'll be fine as long as the door isn't locked."

Stamos shifted his weight from one foot to the other. He looked decidedly uncomfortable. "I'm sorry, Joy, but I'll have to lock you in. It's for your own safety."

Joy swallowed hard, the back of her throat burned. "If I told you I'm innocent?"

"Makes no never mind. It is for your safety."

"Sure, well goodnight then." Joy turned her back on him. She waited a long time until she heard him leave. The door closed and she heard the echo of the lock engaging. Her heart beat faster, she turned and stared at the locked door. The nightmare that was her life, just never ended.

She immediately looked for a way out. The room was windowless. At least she had control over the lights. She planned to keep them on all night. The chill of the night encompassed the little room. Obviously, Stamos forgot that it wasn't heated. Joy grabbed a blanket off the cot and wrapped it around her.

It brought back memories of long days in solitary confinement. Days in which she was sure she'd go mad. All she could think about was her father and brother, waiting for a letter or a visit. She got neither.

The small cot squeaked when she sat on it. Leaning her back against the wall, she pulled the blanket tighter around her. The nights were always the worst. She didn't dare think about her future. There really wasn't a sunny one for her.

Why had George sent her here? She'd been fine, feeling nothing. Now her emotions were scattered. It didn't come as a big surprise that Samos didn't want her. No one did. She was a throw away. She'd been fine with it before coming to the ranch.

Stamos had said that George was sick and she'd be there for a few more days. In some ways, prison was easier. There wasn't this uncertainty. She knew where'd she'd be for the next three years, none of this waiting to see stuff. Her head ached as all her thoughts whirled through her head. She closed her eyes and listened to the night.

*****

Stamos swore as he heard the pounding on his front door. Damn, he'd just gotten back to sleep. Apparently, Bailey's offer to help ended when she went to bed -- alone. Hell, she tried everything to crawl in bed with him. She sure was cute but no, he'd done that with another waitress and somehow he'd gotten her pregnant. Bailey's behavior toward Joy left him with a bad taste in his mouth.

He wiped his hand over his weary face, got up, and pulled on his jeans. Barefoot, he trotted to the door. Kid stood there looking all kinds of sorry. "Out with it," Stamos said impatiently.

"You'd best come, Boss. There's all kinds of wailing like noises comin' from Joy's room. I think she's possessed or somethin'," he said, his eyes bugging out of his head.

Stamos stared at Kid. He shook his head and pulled on his boots. Dillon started crying. "I'll be right there."

Kid nodded and disappeared.

Good God what else? "Hey, buddy." Stamos picked up his son. Bailey must be one heck of a heavy sleeper. "Wanna go outside for a walk? Sure you do." He wrapped him in a quilt.

He walked toward the barn carrying Dillon. Her file didn't mention any mental problems. He wondered what was wrong. Dillon began happily chanting Da Da, Da Da. It warmed Stamos' heart every time.

Knocking on the door, Stamos hoped for a response. He heard her wailing and figured she was having a nightmare. He unlocked the door and peered in. He wasn't going to go in if she looked at all dangerous.

Joy sat up, her hair on end, looking confused. "What happened?"

Stamos heaved a sigh of relief. "You were screaming in your sleep."

Joy's face grew red. "Sorry. I do that sometimes."

Stamos stepped into the room and frowned. "Cold in here isn't it?"

"Yes."

"Awe hell, I'm sorry. I forgot about the space heater. Joy, I'm so sorry. I don't treat people this way."

Joy bit her lip and gazed at him. Nodding her head she simply said, "I know."

Dillon began to fuss, reaching for Joy. "Ma Ma, Ma Ma," he said, wanting her to hold him.

Joy looked at Stamos. "Here, take the little bugger. He's been fussing all night," Stamos said with a smile.

Joy reached out and took Dillon into her arms. The smile she bestowed on Stamos lightened his heart. She'd really taken a hankerin' to Dillon, it was written all over her face.

"Where's Bailey? Did she go home?" Joy asked.

Stamos laughed. "No, she just sleeps through everything."

Joy smiled back at him. Stamos decided to look into her case. He had a hard time believing that she murdered her stepmother.

*****

Joy hugged Dillon. She wasn't too thrilled about the Ma Ma, thing. It was bound to cause trouble, but for that brief moment she closed her eyes and cherished a feeling she had no right to. A feeling that wasn't bound to come her way again, love for and from a child.

When she opened her eyes, Stamos' smile was a surprise. His hat usually covered his jet-black hair, but it hung loose and sexy to his shoulders. The twinkle in his chocolate eyes humbled her. She yearned for the twinkle, but she knew it was for Dillon. It warmed her just the same.

Her gaze lingered on his chest, he'd pulled on a shirt, but he hadn't taken the time to button it. Something stirred inside her at the sight of his hard, muscular chest. Looking lower, she almost gasped at his chiseled abs. She glanced away. Her feelings confused her. She recognized lust and she didn't want it in her life. She'd seen the look of lust many times. She never expected to feel it. Being aloof had been her life for so long. It saved her life many times.

"I'm fine now." She didn't look at him. She knew that she'd turn bright red.

Stamos sat on the bed next to her. His closeness made it hard for her to breathe. She felt so uncomfortable and out of place. She thought that her heart would beat out of her chest.

"Old Dil sure has taken a shine to you."

Joy gave him a brief smile. "I'm sorry, he shouldn't be calling me, Ma Ma. I'm sure he doesn't know what he's saying." Her heart dropped. This would just be one more strike against her.

"That's the rub. If he doesn't know, then he doesn't mean to call me Da Da. Nope, I refuse to believe it. No big deal, he's probably missing Stacey."

"I bet that's it," Joy quickly agreed.

"Come on, let's get you settled on my couch and I'll figure something out for tomorrow night."

Holding Dillon, breathing in his baby scent, Joy followed Stamos. He hadn't acted mad or annoyed. In fact, he gave the impression that he actually cared. Nothing, absolutely nothing was ever as it seemed. She would do well to remember that.

*****

Stamos downed his coffee and poured himself another cup. It'd take the whole pot to keep him awake today. What a night. After he got Joy settled on the couch and Dillon back to sleep, Stamos finally got some shuteye, only to have Joy wake him because Dillon was crying.

It alarmed him that he hadn't heard him. He knew that Joy wouldn't take it upon herself to tend to Dil out of fear of his reaction. He hadn't been so welcoming when she proclaimed her innocence. He felt like an ass, a damn tired ass.

Dillon sat in his highchair. It was a recent development and Dil liked it. He smiled and jabbered watching Stamos all the while. It was an awesome feeling to know that this little being depended on him for everything.

He still took a bottle, but Stamos had started to add baby cereal to Dil's diet. In fact, they were both covered in the gooey stuff.

"Good Morning," Bailey sang out, putting her hand on Stamos' shoulder. "You should have woken me. I could have taken care of Dillon."

Stamos wanted to laugh. At least she was good with Dillon during the day. He'd just have to tough it out until the nanny arrived. "I was up."

Bailey smiled at him. She looked sexy with her just washed corkscrew hair hanging down her back. She had a hot little bod.

"Can I make you breakfast?" she asked.

"No none for me, but fix some for Joy. She had a hard night."

"Where is our little convict? Still locked in her cage?"

"No I'm right here," Joy announced, without a hint of annoyance. She went to the sink, grabbed a clean cloth, wet it, and gently cleaned off Dillon's hands. She went back to the sink to rinse the cloth. She started back toward Dillon. Bailey grabbed the wet cloth out of her hand.

"Don't you dare touch that child. I will not have a convicted murderer touching that innocent baby," Bailey shrieked, causing Dillon to cry.

Joy hesitated for a second, and then she banged out the back door.

"Good riddance to bad rubbish."

"Bailey," Stamos started.

"What? She is a convict."

Stamos sighed. "We'll be back for lunch," he replied, kissing Dillon on the head. "Be good, Dil."

Dillon reached for him. "Da Da, Da Da."

"I'll be back later, buddy," Stamos told him.

He'd call the prosecuting lawyer and see if he could get Joy's court transcripts sent over. Something wasn't right, and he'd blown his chance to find out from Joy.

He pulled his grey Stetson low over his eyes and headed outside. He had horses to train and a few of them were just the right age to start. He had all types of horses. Mostly, he raised quarter horses and paints. He sold many to rodeo riders and cattle ranchers. Lately he'd been having requests for jumpers, and dressage trained horses. First things first, he had a group of foals that needed to learn to wear a head collar and be led in-hand. The real training didn't start until a horse was three years old, but it was important to get them used to humans. Regular handling established trust and confidence.

Stamos watched Joy lead Franklin out of the barn. "Going for a ride?"

"If it's all right with you. I'd like to see what ol' Frankie here can do. He has great conformation. Looks like a real champ."

Stamos frowned and immediately regretted it. Her happiness faded right out of her. "His name is, Franklin. It is in no way shape or form, Frankie."

"Then it's okay if I ride him?"

"Take him for a spin. When you get back you can help me with the foals."

"That's it?" she asked, looking doubtful.

"What's it?"

"I get to just ride away by myself?"

Stamos smiled. "Yes and enjoy yourself."

Her brilliant smile warmed him inside, making him feel on top of the world. He watched in awe as she rode away. She was one hell of a horsewoman. Excellent seat. It was a bit of a disappointment that she'd have to leave soon.

*****

Joy rode until she was out of sight. She halted Frankie, took off her hat, and unbraided her hair. She lifted her face to the bright Texas sun, closed her eyes, and shook her head, enjoying the feel of her hair loose down her back.

"Frankie, lets ride and feel free."

She turned the horse and headed west, loving the feel of the sun at her back as it rose higher into the vast sky. The wind whipped through her hair gloriously. As it hit her face and washed over it, she underwent a cleansing of sorts. Her nerve endings were on high alert and for the first time in eight years, she felt happy to be alive.

Before she knew it, her eyesight grew blurry and her cheeks were wet. Joy's chest heaved as she sobbed. Halting Frankie, she grabbed a bandana out of her back pocket and wiped her eyes.

"Well, Frankie, I guess we should head back. Stamos is probably watching the horizon for us."

Franklin nodded and without any guidance, he turned them and rode for home. Joy knew she was an emotional wreck, but she had work to do and she looked forward to working with the foals.

It was just as she predicted. Stamos stood scanning the horizon and when he spotted them, he stopped, pretending that he hadn't been watching for them.

"Good ride?" he called out to her.

"The best," she replied, trying to smile. "Let me take care of Frank--lin and I'll be right out to help you."

"Sure thing," he called.

Joy could feel his gaze on her the whole time she led Frankie to the barn. The heat from his stare became warm and reassuring. Usually when she sensed someone watching her it wasn't a good thing. She'd become a back against the wall type of person. It served her well, so far.

After grooming Frankie, she let him out into the nearest pasture and joined Stamos. He looked all kinds of tired. "You all right, Boss?"

Stamos gave her a half smile. "Didn't get a whole hell of a lot of sleep last night."

"I know. I'm sorry about that."

"It wasn't just you. It was a combination of Dillon and you. I'll move Dillon in to my room and I have a cot that can be moved into his room that you can use."

"I don't want to cause any trouble."

"It's not a problem, Joy."

The way he said her name warmed her soul. "If you're sure..."

"I'm sure. Now here's my herd of foals, show me what you got."

*****

Joy amazed him. He'd heard it bandied about by his men that she was some type of horse whisperer. He had to give the rumor credence. Even the most skittish of foals allowed her to approach and put the head collar on, along with a lead rope.

It reminded him of Snow White the way animals flocked around her. Joy was a real life Snow White. Animals sensed the goodness in a person. He couldn't take his eyes off her.

He'd almost lost his stoic composure when she rode back in on Franklin with her hair streaming down her back. She was no plain Jane. He knew she tried to be inconspicuous. It's a good strategy for surviving prison. He couldn't believe she thought she could be plain. Her skin glowed from the sun making her look so fresh, so young. Her eyes had a bit of a twinkle in them. A person would have to be blind not to see her beauty. Well, he didn't have any business looking at her that way. She was just a ranch hand.

He glanced at her again and shook his head. No, she was so much more. Stamos wished that he could talk to George about her case. Her files were being sent. He hoped to get them soon.

"Looking good," he called out to her, knowing that she'd take it as good job, but he meant 'looking great in those jeans and love the hair'.

Joy looked at him and smiled. "I love horses."

Her glow drew him to her. He wondered what it would be like to caress her. "It shows."

He thought Bailey was sexy, a one-night stand sexy. Joy, well, he didn't know yet, but she had his interest. Her legs were so long, they were made for wrapping around a man's waist.

It wasn't just her looks that attracted him. She seemed genuine and kind. He found it hard to believe that she was a murderer. She'd been convicted of murder and he needed to keep that foremost in his thoughts until he found out differently. He'd been deceived plenty of times.

Stamos took off his hat and ran his fingers through his hair. Hell, he'd tricked many into believing what he wanted them to believe. He had to admit that he was a great FBI agent. With the right skills, it could be easy to con people. His heart and his head conflicted, not a good sign.

He plunked his hat back on and swore. He needed those damn files.

*****

Joy lay on the cot looking at all the cowboys on the wall border. It ran all round the room at the top of the wall. She liked it, but right now, it made her restless.

She sat up and buried her face in her hands. She could hear Stamos shuffling papers downstairs and she knew what he was looking at. Her heart sank when she recognized the boxes he unloaded from his truck. They were her files. She'd seen them often.

It drove her crazy not knowing which file he was reading now. Was it the crime scene, her confession, or all the manufactured evidence? It didn't matter, it all screamed guilty. Ashamed of her past, a lone tear trailed down her face.

She walked to the door and hesitated. She knew his face would reveal disgust. No matter who read her files, the look was always the same. Part of her wasn't ready to face it, but she had to know.

The lump in her throat caused her to swallow hard. She walked downstairs and stood outside his office door. Taking a few steadying breaths, she knocked. Upon hearing Stamos yell to come in, Joy opened the door and walked in. The lights seemed too bright, shinning on her, resembling a prison tower spotlight. The need to turn and run became overwhelming, but Joy stood her ground.

The look she'd been expecting, the look of disgust, wasn't there. It shook Joy to see a look of sympathy on Stamos' face. She had no recollection of the last time she had seen that expression on anyone's face. She stared at him not knowing what to say or think.

"Joy, take a seat before you fall over," Stamos said gruffly.

Joy obeyed and looked around the room, her trial transcripts were everywhere. She wondered how far he'd gotten. Had he seen the plane ticket purchased in her name with her stepmother's credit card? The jury loved that one. That particular piece of evidence had been the last nail in her coffin.

"Joy?"

"Well I guess I'll be out of here in the morning," she said, sighing.

"Joy, you're shaking."

She gave him a helpless smile. "I can't seem to help it."

Stamos came around the desk, took her hands, and pulled her up until they stood facing each other.

Joy couldn't stand the look in his eyes. Somehow pity hurt worse. Overcome, she looked away.

"Come here," Stamos said softly. He hugged her to him.

Joy stood as wooden as a toy soldier. She didn't remember how to hug. When had she'd been hugged last? She couldn't think. His large comforting hands ran up and down her back, turning her into rubber. Finally, she leaned against him and wrapped her arms around his waist.

The feel of his muscular arms wrapped around her broke her heart. They made her feel safe, but she knew better. After luxuriating in the emotion for another minute, Joy reluctantly pulled away. She couldn't allow herself to feel safe, that's what got you killed.

Chapter Four

Stamos sat behind his heavy oak desk, his gaze never leaving Joy. He noticed the fear on her face and he realized it was a slip on her part. He knew that she had learned to show no fear in prison.

"Eight years is a long time," he said.

She only nodded, looking at the floor. She looked so small in the big leather chair. He hadn't given it much thought before, but this room was distinctly masculine, full of oversized heavy oak and leather furniture.

"You were fourteen and they tried you as an adult?" he asked.

"You have all the information you need right in front of you." Joy tried to sound as though she didn't care, but he wasn't buying it.

"I haven't read it all."

"Yet, you haven't read it all yet." Her hazel eyes flashed at him.

"Do you have a problem with that?" Stamos asked.

Joy shrugged and looked away. "Where's the file on your life story for me to read?" she asked, bitterly.

"Joy, I'm just trying--"

Joy jumped up. "I know what you're trying, Boss. You want to know if I'm going to murder you in your sleep. Let me assure you, this convicted murderer promises not to slit your throat while you sleep."

A gasp at the door made them both turn. Bailey stood there in a silky pink nightgown. "I told you. You can't have her in the house, it just isn't right. I couldn't sleep all night fearing that she might come into my room and do who knows what to me."

Joy rolled her eyes. "You're not my type, honey."

Bailey looked insulted. "Stamos, say something," she demanded.

Stamos stood, walked toward Joy, and put his arm around her shoulders. "Bailey, you don't know the whole story."

"Like you do? Good God, look at all these files. There is no way you read them all tonight." Her voice became louder, bordering on hysterical.

"Bailey, this isn't your business."

"Listen, you two," Joy said, shrugging Stamos' arm off her shoulders. "I'll probably be going back to prison tomorrow. I'm going back to bed."

Stamos watched Joy leave the room. She looked dignified and stoic. Her face had turned to stone, but her eyes gave her away.

"Glad that's over." Bailey smiled at him. Her eyelashes fluttered while she sashayed toward him in her pink nightie. She licked her lips and gave him a smile full of promises.

"Goodnight, Bailey." Stamos escorted her to the door. Despite her protests, he gave her a gentle push out of the room. At the sound of the door locking, he sighed in relief.

Joy didn't want him going through her files. Too bad, he was just sorry that it hurt her. The evidence looked damning, but it also seemed too convenient. There seemed a lot that didn't make sense. He wondered if she still had contact with her father and brother. From what he could tell, they defended her at first, and then they began to find evidence and hand it over to the police one piece at a time.

He heard Dillon begin to fuss. He ran his fingers through his hair. He'd better go get him, Lord knows the sleepless Bailey didn't hear him.

*****

Joy walked into the kitchen. She wished that she could just bypass Stamos and Bailey, especially Bailey. It seemed there was always a Bailey type in her life, someone who wouldn't let the past go.

Joy sensed everyone's gaze turn toward her. It made her face heat up until Dillon reached for her calling, "Ma Ma, Ma Ma, Ma Ma."

Joy smiled, wondering if her face cracked. He looked so adorable, with cereal on his head, waving his sticky hands at her. She intended to give Stamos a brief look, but he had more cereal on his head than Dillon did.

Laughter filled the room and it was hers. Her eyes locked with Stamos' and she laughed even harder at his mock look of outrage. The only one not laughing was Bailey.

"Laugh all you want. You don't have to clean it all up. It'll take a lot of scrubbing to get that boy clean."

Joy took exception to Bailey referring to Dillon as *that boy*. It lacked any type of warmth for Dillon. "Dillon," she said, staring at Bailey.

"What is your problem?" Bailey asked.

"His name is, Dillon, not *that boy*." Joy stared her down.

"Oh for God's sake, get a grip. It doesn't matter what I call him. I still have to scrub him and this kitchen clean," Bailey screeched.

"I'll do it," Joy volunteered.

"When hogs fly. You will not touch that boy you... you... murderer," Bailey shouted, her chest heaving.

"Enough," Stamos demanded.

"I know, I'm sorry. You wouldn't let me touch him anyway." Joy walked to the back door. Pent up frustration made her want to smack Bailey and she knew she had to get out of there. "See you in the barn, Boss."

Stepping out into the cool morning air, Joy took a deep breath. It would never get old, wide-open spaces made her feel free. She never should have taken on Bailey. She'd be sent away for sure.

She understood that she couldn't change anything, she never could. She walked to the barn. Animals were a refuge for her. She understood them and they understood her.

To her surprise, she found a grey mare and a little filly in the barn. The mare was greeting the horses. Joy laughed, momentarily forgetting her troubles. "Now where did you come from?" she asked, approaching the pair.

"That's Nanny and Nino," Benji told her.

Ever since their first meeting when he tried to come on to her, he'd been her gentle giant. No one messed with her as long as Benji was around.

Joy sent Benji a big smile. "Hello, Nanny, hello, Nino," she said, approaching them. She patted Nanny on the head. "This must be your baby. She is very pretty."

Benji giggled. "She don't know what you're sayin', Joy."

"Sure she does. Look, she's smiling."

"Yeah she is. You are wonderful, Joy," Benji enthused, reaching out and pettimg Nanny.

"Now, where did she come from?" Joy asked.

"Hey, Nanny. Is that you?" Stamos asked, his voice booming.

"Yes, Boss, and little Nino too," Benji told him, happily.

"Okay, who is Nanny? Why haven't I seen her before?"

"Nanny is the Houdini of horses. You can lock her in, but she always gets out. She enjoys making the rounds of the local ranches, letting herself into barns and stalls. She even has a favorite Billy goat friend that escapes and follows her."

"The Boss is right, she is a wonder horse," Benji said.

"This is the first time she's brought her daughter Nino here for a visit," Stamos told Joy. He turned toward Nanny and patted her withers. "You did good, girl. Look at your filly all black and grey. She's a beauty the same as you. I bet she's just as smart."

Nanny nodded her head and Joy was beside herself. "Now this is a horse I could whisper to all day long."

Joy took the moment to stare her fill at Stamos. His skin appeared deeply tanned, but there was a copper undertone. His face looked as chiseled as his body. He had high cheekbones and smile lines that were so deep that Joy got the impression that he loved life. An impulse to touch his silky black hair ran though her. It scared her. These were feelings she never allowed herself before.

So lost in thought, Joy hadn't noticed that Stamos was staring back at her. It startled her. Too bad his view wasn't as pleasing as hers was. She knew she wasn't much to look at, and that was her ultimate goal.

"Do I still have baby food on my head?" Stamos asked, looking amused.

"What? Oh no, I was just wool gathering. So where are these two beauties from?"

"Nanny lives at the O'Neill ranch. Hasn't been around much since she's become a mama." Stamos turned and looked at Nanny. "You came to show off your pretty daughter, right?"

Nanny nodded her head.

Joy laughed. "Is the O'Neill ranch close?"

"They are our closest neighbors. Good people, Callie and Garrett. I worked on their ranch for a time."

"I thought you were a lawman?" Joy asked.

"I was, it was an undercover operation, but it made me realize that ranching is in my blood. I grew up on a ranch."

Inner warmth gifted Joy. No one shared personal things with her. "I'll get to mucking out the stalls. Nanny, it was nice to meet you and your little Nino."

Joy got the shovel and wheel barrel while Benji led the paint into the corral. She didn't mind mucking out stalls. Anything to do with horses and she was all for it. The morning was quite cool, but she had no problem working up a sweat.

She heard voices at the barn entrance. She glanced and turned away. It couldn't be. She knew there was no mistake. It was her brother. Quickly she looked for another way out. The voices were growing louder and she wanted to hide in a stall with her hands over her ears. Pain lanced through her body. Why now? Why here?

Fear seized her heart as she stared at Jamie. He'd grown into a man these last eight years. Clearly not a nice man, he cursed at Stamos. Joy watched Stamos escort Jamie away. The pain of her brother's betrayal and rejection had cut her to pieces.

She tried to feel numb, but tears pricked at the back of her eyes. The pain was too much to bear, even now. There was no getting past the pain of her family's actions. Joy had thought that she and Jamie were close, but it was all smoke and mirrors. He'd been saying hurtful things, vile things behind her back. She wouldn't have believed it, not of her Jamie, but she overheard him one night saying he couldn't stand to be in the same room as her.

To this day, she wasn't privy to what she'd done to him. Jamie was reminiscent of the head of a snake -- he quickly turned and bit, leaving a poison of pain inside her.

Even after all he'd done, she'd tried to reach out to him. Phone calls were rejected. He'd been the ultimate betrayer and she'd been pathetic trying to hold on.

She shoveled the hay, trying to get her mind off her problems. She turned and ended up dumping a shovelful of manure at Stamos' feet. Joy couldn't look at him. She could only imagine what her brother had said about her this time. It shamed her. "I'm sorry."

"Joy, look at me," Stamos cajoled, "Joy, he's a jerk. I know he's your brother, but I don't allow uninvited visits here."

Joy nodded and went back to work. At any minute, she might fly into a million pieces.

"Joy, please look at me."

Joy put down the shovel and turned. The compassion in Stamos' face appeared welcoming. When he opened his arms to her, she walked into them and put her face in his shoulder, crying.

"Are you crying because I sent him away?"

"No," she managed to choke out.

"Good, he's a first class ass."

Stamos' hands rubbed up and down her back comforting her. She closed her eyes and breathed in his scent. Old Spice, she knew because it was on the bathroom counter. He smelled so good. Maybe when this nightmare was all over she'd buy herself a bottle to remember him by. She wished that she had the nerve to snuggle against him. It wouldn't be right. Looking over his shoulder, she spotted both Benji and Bailey staring at them. Benji looked positively giddy while Bailey shot her daggers with her eyes.

Joy pulled away from Stamos and nodded her head toward their audience.

"Benji are all the stalls taken care of?" Stamos asked.

"Yep, Boss. Do I get to hug Joy next?" he asked.

"No, I need you to check on Franklin."

"Your horse? You got it, Boss," Benji said, happily.

Stamos turned his gaze to Bailey. "Where's Dillon?"

"Sleeping, I just wanted to know who the tall handsome man was, but now I also want to know if you are sleeping with the criminal?"

"No one important, and of course I'm not. Please go check on Dillon."

Looking annoyed, Bailey shrugged her shoulders and slowly walked away.

The smile he bestowed on Joy made her heart beat faster and her pain lessened. It didn't go away, but it lessened for now. No one had ever been able to do that for her and it made her try to smile in return.

"He won't be back," Stamos told her.

"Is that one of your rules?"

"No, I read a lot of the trial transcripts last night. I hate to say this, but your brother is scum."

"But..." Joy started.

Stamos drew her back into the circle of his strong arms. He kissed her on the side of her forehead. "I'm not done reading, but honey, I think you've been all types of wronged."

Joy pulled back and looked at him. She had to see his eyes. She had to know he was sincere. No one had believed her in such a long time and she couldn't believe it now.

"I think you should stay at the ranch and work your program. You don't deserve to be sent back."

Stunned, Joy stared at him. She still stared as he let her go and walked out of the barn.

*****

Joy took off her Stetson and wiped her brow. Her muscles ached with exhaustion. She missed lunch, on purpose, and the hunger gnawed at her stomach. She didn't want to see Bailey. Lord only knew what Jamie had said to her. Her spirit was crushed and she wasn't in the mood for Bailey's games.

She opened the door and found Dillon waving his hands in the air crying. Bailey ignored him. Joy immediately picked him up and cooed to him. He began to babble Ma Ma, Ma Ma.

"Put that boy down or I will slice you with this knife," Bailey warned, her face contorted.

Stunned, Joy stared at Bailey. It was similar to being in prison again. Slowly, she put Dillon back into his highchair. He began to wail and Joy hoped it would bring Stamos. Bailey still held the knife and her look of hatred scared Joy. She'd been stabbed before and she wasn't about to let it happen again.

"Bailey, what are you thinking?" she asked, while her mind whirled looking for a way out.

Bailey smiled at her and turned back to cooking. Stunned, Joy didn't know what to do. She walked past a crying Dillon, grabbed him, and went to her room to change.

Closing the door, she leaned against it breathing hard. It brought flashbacks of prison life. Bailey had problems. Something wasn't right about her. Joy wished that she could tell Stamos, but she didn't want him to be sorry that he'd let her stay on the ranch.

"Joy? I'll take Dillon." Stamos' voice was loud through the door. He turned the knob and she stepped back.

"Here." She handed Dillon to him.

"Is everything all right? Bailey said he'd been fussy and you were helping out."

She stilled her surprise and shook her head. "Everything is fine."

"Well good, dinner in a few."

Joy nodded as Stamos closed the door behind him. She wondered what Bailey's game was.

She changed and walked toward the kitchen. It seemed quiet. She didn't hear Dillon crying. She almost walked into the kitchen, but she stopped short. Stamos was holding Dillon and Bailey in his arms. Joy's heart skipped a beat. Quietly she left through the front door.

She felt gut kicked by what she had seen, but she had to admit that they made a nice looking family. He'd been kind to her and somehow she turned it into more. She'd let her guard down and she couldn't afford to again. Stamos didn't know how dangerous Bailey could be, but she knew it would be her word against Bailey's. She never won.

Navigating outside prison proved to be just as tricky as inside, perhaps more so. There she learned the rules quickly. Here, she wasn't so sure what the rules even were.

It surprised her to find Kid sitting on the top rung of the corral fence. He smiled and waved her over. "Nothing compares to wide open spaces," he commented.

Joy looked into his brown eyes. She could sense his pain. "A person could get used to it," she responded.

"Hear tell you're stayin'," he drawled in a heavy Texas accent.

"That's what the Boss says."

"He's a good man. He knows where we're coming from. He did six months undercover in the Pen. He always seems to know how to handle us."

"Do most people stay on after the program?" Joy swung up onto the fence rung and sat next to Kid.

"I've been here a year. Most men have families and other obligations. Benji and Corny are lifers though."

"I've been meaning to ask. What happened to Benji?"

"He was hit in the head by a guard, made him mental like. He's a good enough guy."

"What was he in prison for?"

"He masterminded the greatest bank robberies of this century -- well make that last century. We've all been gone for a while. Now he has trouble tying his shoes. He's loyal to Stamos. Don't know what they would have done with him if Stamos hadn't insisted that he come live on the ranch."

"I'm glad he has a home."

"Hear tell you were in for murder. Is it true?"

Joy sighed. Everyone always wanted the details. "Something like that," she said. "I'll see you in the morning."

"Goodnight, Joy."

Joy nodded and walked toward the house. She learned a few nice things about Stamos. She dreaded seeing them all together. She took a deep breath and opened the door.

Bailey stood there looking blazing mad. "What did you tell him, you little whore?"

Joy quickly looked to see if Bailey had a knife on her. "I don't know what you mean," she said, trying to step around Bailey.

"Oh no you don't," Bailey hissed, blocking Joy's way. "Stamos has a bug in his ear about how I treat you. I'm asking again, what did you say to him?"

Joy just stared at her.

"Don't think I didn't see you out there rubbing up against Kid. I know everything that goes on around here. I even know that your trashy brother plans to get to you one way or the other." Bailey crossed her arms and smiled.

Joy had no idea what Bailey's problem was. All she knew was that Bailey was crazy. "Well thanks for the info, now if you'll let me by, I'd like to get some shut eye."

Stamos stepped out into the hall. "What's going on here?"

"Ask *her*," Joy said, her tone heated.

"She was outside with Kid getting naked, if you know what I mean. I told you she was a whore. She needs to go," Bailey yelled.

Joy walked away. No one ever believed her before and she wasn't about to stand there and see Bailey gloat. No one called her back as she climbed the stairs and she wasn't sure if she should be relieved or insulted.

She walked into her room and found a soft flowered nightgown on her bed. Sitting on the bed, she touched it and smiled. It was the most feminine thing she'd ever gotten. The softness of the cotton made her smile. In an instant, she changed.

Hearing Dillon cry in the next room, Joy didn't know if she should try to help or not. The crying went on for a bit and Joy's decision was made for her. She couldn't stand to hear him cry.

*****

Stamos watched Joy from the doorway. She looked lovely in her new gown and her hair unbraided. What a natural she was with Dillon. Joy filled his heart and he almost laughed at his own thoughts. She worked for him. That's all.

Her eyes widened when she spotted him. "It's fine, Joy."

"I didn't think you wanted me near him, but he was crying."

"You're good with him."

Joy smiled and once again, Stamos was amazed at how beautiful her smile looked.

"Thank you for the nightgown." She ducked her head looking at the floor.

Stamos chuckled at the redness of her face. "First one I ever bought, looks right pretty."

"Thanks," she murmured.

The atmosphere became awkward. "Well he looks like he's sleeping now."

Joy looked at him. "Oh yes. I'll put him in his crib."

Stamos watched her. She was as good with children as she was with horses. "About what Bailey said..."

Joy turned from the crib. "I didn't. I..."

"I know that. Bailey's jealous. She's husband hunting."

A tear rolled down her face.

"Joy?" Stamos inquired, stepping in front of her.

"I'm sorry. I don't cry. It's just that no one has believed a word out of my mouth in a long time," she whispered.

"Joy?" Stamos took her into his arms. Their eyes met and he could see her need. He leaned down and kissed her. Her lips were soft and sweet and he wanted more. Licking the seam of her lips, she opened for him. She seemed inexperienced somehow. At last, she opened to him and he explored her mouth with his tongue. His hands landed on her delectable rear end, pulling her closer.

Her responses seemed genuine yet tentative. Then it hit him. It could be that she hadn't kissed anyone this way before. Stamos pulled away, looked into her passion filled eyes, and gazed at her red ruby lips. She looked dazed.

"What's wrong?" she asked.

"Nothing, honey," Stamos said, taking a step back and dropping his hands from her. "It's just not right. You work here and I can't take advantage of you."

A look of confusion crossed her face. "I understand," she said softly. "I'd better go to bed."

"Goodnight, Joy."

Joy didn't look at him. She paused at the door and murmured a quick goodnight and left.

*****

Joy sat on her bed. Her entire body tingled. She needed to unbind her breasts. They ached. She pulled the soft gown over her head and unleashed them from the tight ace bandage. It felt freeing. Maybe it was time to stop wearing it.

Joy pulled her gown back on and once again, she stroked the soft cotton, awed that Stamos had bought it for her. She was reading too much into the gift and the kiss.

It'd been her first kiss and she intended to cherish the moment forever. She knew the score, being a convicted murderer did not put her in the running for Stamos' girlfriend, wife, or mother to Dillon.

A sharp pain pinged her heart, admitting it now would save her from more hurt. Both Stamos and Dillon were wriggling their way into her thoughts, and her heart, and she needed to put a stop to it. She knew she could. She'd been cold and unfeeling when it had mattered.

Tears pricked at the back of her eyes and she swore. She refused to cry. She was a hardened criminal and she wouldn't cry. One lone tear trailed down her cheek. Impatiently she wiped it away and got into bed. Lightly touching her lips she sighed, then fell asleep.

Chapter Five

Once again, she bound her breasts, but it seemed harder to do. Joy could have sworn she heard more than one child downstairs. Curious, she dressed quickly. She didn't own a bra and she wouldn't until she summoned the nerve to ask Stamos to buy one.

As she hurried down the stairs, Joy was pleased to see not one but three children. Two she didn't know, but they sure could run -- in different directions. Their lighthearted play touched her.

A beautiful blond scurried after one and called to Joy to wrangle the other. Joy laughed as she tried to corner the little blond girl. She resembled her mother. The toddler shrieked and giggled, as she ran circles around Joy.

The blond woman caught her up and kissed her. "Rose I need you to eat," she said, with loving affection.

"I'm Callie by the way," the woman yelled, over the noise. She strapped Rose into a highchair and sighed in relief. "They keep me thin. I'm always running after them and they never go in the same direction," she told Joy, smiling.

"Where's Bailey?" Joy asked.

"I sent her packing. I can't believe she was here as long as she was. If I had known..." Callie glanced at her. "She wasn't a friend of yours was she?"

Joy shook her head. "No, she hates me."

Callie put out three bowls of rice cereal. "She isn't a fan of mine either. Here, I hope you're willing." She gave Joy a bowl for Dillon. "I can handle Rose and Aidan, but three -- it's pushing it. It'll be an interesting day."

"I'm Joy." She took the bowl and sat next to Dillon's high chair.

"Ma Ma, Ma Ma, Ma Ma," he yelled happily, reaching for her.

"How cute," Callie commented.

Joy could feel her face growing warm. She was certain she looked tomato red. Leaning over, she kissed Dillon on the cheek. Her emotions were all twisted. "Let's get you fed, buddy."

"Does that include me?" Stamos asked.

Callie got up and kissed his cheek. "Let me get these little rascals fed then I'll get your breakfast."

Joy watched Stamos pull Callie close and hug her. "Thanks for being here."

"Not a problem, cowboy. Hey I noticed that Nanny and Nino are here."

"Yep, they like Joy. You might not get them back," Stamos teased.

Callie grinned at Joy. "Well if they like her better..."

Joy tried to spoon the cereal into Dillon's mouth. So far, it was on his cheek, in his ear, and in his hair. "How do you do this?" she asked Stamos.

Stamos laughed. "I usually have it all over me. At least you aim in the right direction," he teased.

Joy admired his smiling face and went back to feeding Dillon. She enjoyed Stamos' smiles too much. She had to admit that it was much more pleasant without Bailey glaring at her. She liked Callie.

She finally had an empty bowl. How much Dillon ate, she had no idea. Joy grabbed a clean cloth and gently wiped him off, talking to him in baby talk the whole time.

Her heart swelled when Dillon reached for her again and yelled, "Ma Ma Ma."

Joy peeked at Stamos out of the corner of her eye. He nodded to her, and she happily unhooked the safety strap and took Dillon into her arms. He gurgled and chanted. "Ma Ma."

"I don't know why he calls me that," she told Stamos and Callie apologetically.

"I think it's wonderful," Callie enthused.

Joy watched as Stamos shot Callie a warning look. "Joy, can you help Callie out for a few before we start with the foals again?"

Joy looked at Callie, unsure of what to say.

"We women will be just fine without a big strong man to help with the diapers," Callie said with laughter in her voice.

Stamos stood up, kissed Callie on the cheek, and then stepped toward Joy. He leaned down and kissed Dillon, but he stared at her.

Joy's heart began to pound. She didn't know what the look meant. It was a nice look, a piercing look, hell she didn't know. She didn't have the experience to know.

"Well, Joy, I for one am glad you are here. You are just what Stamos and Dillon need," Callie praised.

"I doubt that. If you knew..."

"Already know enough. Stamos filled me in on how you got railroaded before I came over."

Surprise filled Joy. "He said that?"

Callie smiled. "He sure did. Now let's get these munchkins into a bath so that you can go cowboying."

"Do you think it's unfeminine?"

"Don't even say it. You are looking at the best roper in the county. I'm on a horse chasing down cattle every chance I get."

Joy laughed. "Probably not much time for that."

"Well, luckily I have my Garrett. He knows if I don't ride the ranch every once in a while I go stir crazy. He's really great. Oh, I wanted to ask what size you wear. Stamos mentioned that he had to give you men's undies to wear."

Joy flushed. "I need a bra," she said, showing Callie a glimpse of her binding.

Callie looked at her chest and laughed. "Doesn't that hurt?"

"It's uncomfortable, but necessary in prison if you can get away with it."

"Come on, let's get these babies cleaned and dressed then we can figure out sizes and what else you need."

*****

The next morning, Joy looked at herself in the mirror. She wore a new, light blue tee shirt and a bra. The sight before her astounded her. She knew that her breasts were big, but good Lord, she never envisioned looking close to this.

Taking a deep breath, she went to the kitchen. Callie would be there again, and then tomorrow she was going to take Dillon to her house for the day. The new nanny had been promised for tomorrow afternoon. Joy hoped for a grandmotherly type, but anyone would be better than Bailey.

Garrett, Callie's husband, held both twins on his lap. His handsome face looked animated. Joy smiled. Callie was one lucky woman.

"Breakfast is ready," Callie called, as she sat to feed Dillon.

"Can I feed him?" Joy asked.

Callie gave her a brilliant smile. "Have at it, I have to rescue my husband."

Both woman looked over and laughed, watching the twins trying to pull on Garrett's ears.

"Hey, a little help?" Garrett asked, his blue eyes twinkling.

Joy watched in envy as Callie went to his rescue. They looked so happy. Soon enough she was distracted by Dillon hitting his hands on the tray of the high chair chanting, "Ma Ma, Ma Ma."

"Okay, little man, let's get you fed," Joy said.

She didn't hear Stamos enter, but she could feel his stare. Suddenly she remembered her breasts. She glanced at him and knew what he was staring at and it wasn't her widened eyes. Embarrassed, she hunched over and continued to feed Dillon.

"How do you do that?" Stamos asked.

Joy flushed. "Do what?" she asked, without looking up.

"Feed Dillon without getting it in your hair?" Stamos asked, with a hint of laughter in his voice.

Darting her eyes at him again, she wasn't sure if he was laughing at her. "Takes practice."

"You look nice this morning," he commented, grabbing a strip of bacon.

"What's that supposed to mean?" All men were identical.

"Whoa, it's a compliment."

"Oh? Really? Why now?" she asked, suspiciously.

"What's wrong with giving you a compliment?" Stamos asked.

Joy stood up and pointed to her chest. "This is what's wrong. The bane of my existence. If you want to stare then stare and get it out of your system."

Looking around the room, she noticed bewildered looks on all their faces. Barely holding back a sob, she grabbed her coat and rushed out the door.

She expected to hear laughter, but all she heard was Callie telling Stamos to let her be.

*****

Stamos knew he'd stepped in it. The shock of seeing how well-endowed she'd suddenly become took him by surprise. He wasn't the type of man who degraded woman. Well, he hadn't before, now he felt awful. Callie explained how Joy had bound her breast and just how painful it must have been.

He slapped his hat against his thigh, then looked up at the big Texas sky. He'd have to apologize, but how could he apologize without sticking his foot in his mouth?

Shaking his head, he headed toward the pasture where Joy was working with Nino at Nanny's insistence. Yesterday Nanny pushed Nino to the front of the herd of foals that were to be lead around using the head collar. Joy had taken it in stride, but Stamos was amazed. Nino wasn't even his horse.

"Pretty little filly isn't she?" he asked, walking closer to Joy. So far, she hadn't acknowledged him.

"A smart one too, she takes after her mother," Joy responded, paying all of her attention to Nino.

"Joy, about this morning. I well, I... Hell, I'm sorry. I don't know how to apologize without bringing the whole thing up so-- I'm sorry."

Joy seemed flustered. "It's fine. I've caused quite a stir around here this morning. Benji had tears in his eyes as he turned me toward all the men and told them that I had turned into a woman."

Stamos couldn't help it, he laughed, deep and long. "I'm... I'm sorry," he said, between bouts of laughter.

Nanny came over and head butted him.

"Thanks, Nanny." Joy walked off leading Nino.

Stamos tried to be serious, but hell it was gut bustin' funny. He turned and walked toward the barn. He knew he was going to laugh again and he didn't want to do it within hearing distance of Joy.

*****

The shadows of late afternoon began to engulf the ranch. Joy sat just outside the barn on an old wooden bench. It'd been a long day. The horses were wonderful, the human's not so much. All day she'd been fighting the urge to run into the house and bind her breasts. She'd tried so hard for so long to be invisible and now she'd become the center of attention.

Twirling a piece of hay between her fingers, she became lost in thought. Stamos sat next to her and she never heard his approach. She was losing her edge and it couldn't happen.

"Long day," Stamos commented.

"If you say so."

"Joy, I'm sorry. I should have been more sensitive. Instead I acted like a first class jackass and I've been kicking myself about it all day."

Joy turned her head and gave him a long steady look. He seemed sincere. "It's fine."

"No. It isn't fine, Joy. You don't have to just go with the flow and accept everything that comes along. You're not in prison."

She nodded her head and turned away. "It's hard to change eight years of habits, habits that kept me alive."

"Joy, I know how it is in prison, it's brutal. When did you go? When you turned eighteen or twenty-one?"

"Fourteen."

Stamos looked shocked. "I mean adult prison."

Joy gave him a sad smile. "I know, they tried me as an adult and sent me to the state penitentiary."

"How the hell did that happen?"

"It's a long story. It wasn't supposed to go down that way. Funny thing, once they locked me up, my family never came to see me. Not once. They wouldn't accept my phone calls and they returned my mail. They left me to rot all alone."

Stamos put his arm around her and pulled her close to his side. "Which one did you cover for? Was it your father or your brother?"

Wide eyed, Joy stared at Stamos. "What are you talking about?"

"Hey, don't panic. I know you didn't kill anyone."

Joy closed her eyes and sighed. "You're wrong."

Stamos stood up and paced in front of Joy. His eyes looked stormy and it looked as though he was gathering his thoughts. "I know you didn't do it. I'm pretty sure I know who did it. What I can't understand is why you won't tell me."

Joy looked away. Stamos' eyes looked into her soul and she couldn't allow that. She'd made her decision eight long years ago and she couldn't go back. The thought of telling the truth terrified her and it would just put Stamos in danger. "You're wrong. I hated my stepmother so I took a knife and slit her throat while she slept."

"Joy, look at me," Stamos said, his voice demanding.

Joy couldn't look at him. "It is what it is, Stamos."

"Joy?"

Joy turned her head and gave him her most intimidating stare. "Drop it."

Stamos looked frustrated, but he nodded his head. "If that's what you want."

"It's what I need." She drank in the sight of him. He'd send her back now. He wouldn't have a choice. "I'll pack my things," she said, as she stood.

Stamos grabbed her hand. "I'm not releasing you from the program. No matter what, you're still the best horse trainer I've ever seen. You'll work your three years."

Joy looked down at her work worn hand in his hard-callused one. His so big and strong and hers so small, but just as strong. "Thank you," she whispered.

"Joy?"

Joy put her fingers over his sexy lips. "Please, Stamos, don't ask me what I can't tell you."

Stamos' gaze never left hers as he leaned down and brushed her lips with his. Joy shivered in delight and stepped closer to him. He brushed her lips again, making her want more. Stamos deepened the kiss and Joy smiled against his mouth. It felt wonderful and she didn't want it to end.

She reached up and wrapped her arms around his strong neck. Her soft breasts pushed against his hard muscled chest. Sighing, she opened her mouth to him. The tingling of her body started slow, but then her whole body filled with electric pulses. This is what she'd missed her whole life. He made her feel things she couldn't have comprehended before. It was heaven just touching another human being, but Stamos excited her beyond anything she'd ever experienced. She moaned and pressed herself against him.

Suddenly she heard Dillon's cry coming from Stamos' side. She pulled away confused.

Stamos smiled. "Baby monitor. We'd better go see what his highness needs." He grabbed her hand.

Joy looked at their linked hands and followed him. She was never more thrilled, confused, or terrified. Secretly she hoped that Dillon called her Ma Ma.

Chapter Six

It'd been a hectic morning. Callie dropped by to pick up Dillon, and Stamos packed every conceivable item that Dillon might need. Callie laughed and Joy watched in envy as Stamos kissed Callie's cheek.

The kiss Joy had shared with Stamos the night before had been too brief. After he took care of Dillon, Stamos had ignored her and closed himself up in his office. Joy didn't know what to think, but she knew the bite of rejection. It seemed obvious that Stamos regretted his actions. He regretted their spine tingling kiss.

Joy decided that she wasn't going to kiss him anymore. She wanted to enjoy being free. There were so many little things each day that made her spirit soar, and she didn't need the drama of Stamos to ruin it.

So far today, a monarch butterfly made her spirit soar. She watched it fly free and she felt a bit lost. She took a deep breath, and prepared to muck out the stalls.

"You won't need the shovel today," Stamos called to her from the yard.

Joy stood still watching him walk toward her. His muscles showed through his shirt and his jeans were tight, outlining his muscled thighs. Her heart beat faster. Her mind and body were not working in tandem. She couldn't seem to help herself. She found him attractive.

"I want Benji to show you the ranch. You've been stuck in this barn long enough."

"I don't mind," she protested.

Stamos smiled a deep smile. His eyes twinkled. "Go get Franklin and I'll find Benji. He loves to be a tour guide."

Joy grinned at Stamos, nodded her head, and turned around to saddle Frankie. She could feel the warmth of his gaze on her back.

It felt glorious to ride the range. The wind whipped against her face and through her hair. Joy experienced an excitement she hadn't known since childhood. It was going to be a great day. Benji was a great rider and an even better tour guide.

He was so good that Joy wished that he'd stop talking occasionally. Stamos owned a beautiful piece of land and she could see why he was so proud. Suddenly, she heard a baleful cry of a cow and they turned their horses.

Franklin rode straight toward the ailing cow. She was down in a ravine with no way out. The sides going down were straight up and down, too vertical to get down to her.

"I could go down," Benji volunteered.

"No, Benji, it would be suicide. We need to look at it from all angles."

"What?" Benji asked.

"Get down and we'll walk along the ridge of the ravine. She must have walked down there, she's not hurt. If she'd fallen in, she'd have a broken leg."

"Joy, you are so smart."

Joy winked at her giant friend. "Let's get walking."

Still, it was steep.

"We can't get a horse down there."

"I could rope her and help her find her way," Benji suggested.

Joy was doubtful that Benji could do it, but it was that or nothing. "Let's give it a try."

Benji's prowess with a rope amazed her. He roped the cow in one try. Joy talked soothingly to the poor animal as Benji and his horse Monroe, pulled her.

The cow lost her footing a few times, but Benji got her out. "Benji, you are wonderful," Joy praised.

"Yep I know," he replied, with a smile.

They led the cow toward the right direction and let her go. Joy was on the top of the world until an ATV came toward them. As far as she knew, Stamos didn't use them. Both horses became agitated as it came closer.

"Wonder who that is?" Benji commented, not at all worried.

"I don't know," Joy said.

The ATV came closer and it slowed. Joy and Benji sat on their horses. As the rider got off, Joy gasped. It was her father.

He hadn't aged much. He still looked akin to a huge man not to be crossed. His dark, straight hair with a touch of gray was the only change that Joy could detect. It surprised her that he looked just the same as he did eight years ago.

"Landed on your feet," he drawled as he walked closer. He stopped a few feet away.

"I'm a cat. I have nine lives," Joy said sharply.

"I know, used up about seven of them if my count is right," he said, his words sounded flippant but Joy knew better.

"Must be one I didn't know about. There were only six attempts on my life while I rotted away in prison."

"Could be I counted wrong." He shrugged.

"Benji, this is Wood Courtland. He's supposed to be my father, but I'm still hoping for that little fact to be untrue."

Benji just stared at the big man.

Joy gazed at her father. If he said there were seven attempts then there were. Something must have foiled his plan. Someone other than her for a change. "What are you doing here?"

"I wanted to see my baby girl," Wood said, smiling.

"Like hell. Tell me what you want or Benji here will take care of you."

Benji looked at her in surprise then squinted his eyes at Wood. "You'd better believe it, mister," he said in an over the top menacing voice.

"I don't want any trouble. I just wanted to send you a message. Don't think about opening your mouth. Your boss is snooping around and I'd hate to have to burn him out," Wood said, in a singsong voice.

"Get off this land," Joy warned.

Benji jumped off his horse and marched menacingly toward Wood. Wood ran for the ATV and sped off. "I'm sorry, Joy."

"Benji, you were magnificent. You had my back just like a cowboy should. I'm proud of you."

"So you're not mad?"

"No, let's make tracks for home. I'm hungry." She tried to sound light hearted. Inside she quaked. Her heart beat fast and she became light headed. What should she do? The best thing, she decided, was to discourage Stamos from looking into her case.

The sweet memory of his kiss tore her in two. Somehow, Stamos had gotten past her stone cold heart. What if something happened to Dillon? She would never forgive herself. With a heavy heart, and broken dreams, she rode for the ranch house.

*****

Stamos watched as the pair as rode in. Benji looked pleased with himself and it made Stamos smile. "How'd it go?"

"I done scared me a varmint," Benji said, excitedly.

Stamos shot Joy a look of askance but she looked away. "What happened?"

"A man on a tractor came and said mean things to Joy so I stomped him," Benji told him, jumping down from the horse.

Stamos turned to Joy, who stood unmoving next to Franklin. "Tell me that there is not an injured person on my ranch," he thundered, taking a step toward Joy.

"No. Unfortunately Benji didn't get that close." Joy tried to brush past Stamos.

Stamos grabbed her arm. "You, my dear, are not going anywhere until you explain to me what happened."

Joy looked down at his hand on her arm. She tried to pull away, but Stamos held firm. He knew that if she wanted, she could get away. Fighting in prison was dirty.

"Benji, take care of the horses."

"Sure, Boss." He took the reins from Joy. "Don't forget to tell him how I saved the day."

Joy smiled at him." I'll tell him what a hero you are, Benji. Thank you for taking care of me."

Benji puffed out his chest and led both horses away.

"Let's go to the house where I can interrogate you in peace." He reined in his temper making his voice sound a *let's go have tea* cordial.

"Well at least you're a straight shooter. Interrogate. Yep, I do believe that is what you'll do."

Stamos was silent as they walked to the house. He noticed that Joy tried to seem calm, but she wasn't. He could tell she was agitated.

He motioned for her to sit in the chair in front of his desk as he sat in the one behind it. Taking a deep breath, he studied her. She had her tough badass look on her face, but he knew better. In fact, her eyes had a look of hurt in them.

"It was my father. He drove up on an ATV. He had a message for me, Benji jumped off his horse and my father left. Not much to tell."

Stamos shook his head amazed. "Not much to tell? Sounds to me there is a whole lot to tell."

"Not really," Joy countered.

"Yes really," Stamos replied. He was enjoying himself.

Joy's eyes narrowed. "It was just my father."

"Do you mean the one who never visited you in all eight years you were in prison?"

Joy looked away. "The very same."

Stamos didn't know what to make of Joy. She didn't want to talk about it, but hell it happened on his land and someone could have been hurt. "I have a right to know everything that happened out there."

Joy got up and went to the window. Stamos could see her body shaking as she stood looking out. "I'll just call the authorities and have them sort it out."

Joy turned and gave him a wild, wide-eyed look. "No. Please, Stamos, you have to stop looking into my case. I did it. I'm guilty, so leave it be."

Stamos backed off. He could see the terror in her eyes. "I'll leave you be. I have to go pick up Dillon."

Stamos grabbed the keys to his truck and walked out of the house. He was more determined than ever to find out what happened the night her stepmother was killed.

*****

Joy held Dillon and stared out the window. A car drove up the drive and Joy hoped it had the new housekeeper in it. Stamos hadn't said much to her. He barely looked at her last night and this morning he put Dillon in her arms and ran out saying that he had a meeting in town.

Joy held her breath, waiting to see how the other woman looked. To her immense relief she was a wonderfully rounded person. Her gray hair made Joy relax. A nice difference from Bailey. Joy felt optimistic.

Joy opened the door and before she knew it, Dillon was in the other woman's arms babbling at her, telling her the story of his life.

"Call me, Bea. What a charmer this little one is. Oh, love, what is your name?"

"His name is Dillon," Joy responded, feeling more comfortable by the minute.

"I meant your name, love."

"I'm Joy."

The blue-eyed woman smiled. "Tis a beautiful name for sure. I'm glad to meet you, Joy. I'm hoping that this works out for all of us. I just know I could be happy here tending this grand house and taking care of this little tinker."

Joy wondered where she was from. Her lilting accent was one that Joy wasn't familiar with. Joy wasn't about to ask. She'd learned not to.

"Well, love, do you think you could give me a wee tour and then I'll be right at home," Bea said, kissing Dillon's head. "A more beautiful babe there never was."

Joy liked Bea immediately. Hopefully there would be no tension with Bea in the house. Joy showed her around. Bea oohed and aahed at the littlest things. Joy became enchanted with her.

"Is Mr. Walker out working?" They ended the tour in the kitchen.

"He went to Lasso Springs."

"Well, love, why don't you entertain little Dilly here while I whip up lunch? I can't have you leave until I get the Mister's okay. The easiest way to find yourself without a job is to presume things you shouldn't."

Joy smiled, advice to live by. The more she knew Bea, the more she approved of her.

Dillon smiled and smiled. He liked Bea too, but soon enough he was looking at Joy saying, "Ma Ma, Ma Ma."

"The little darling knows his Ma that's for sure." Bea placed grilled chicken and a salad in front of Joy.

Joy's face grew red. "I'm not..."

"He thinks you are." Bea poured sweet tea into a glass.

Joy's heart opened and she needed to slam it shut, but before she had the chance Stamos walked into the kitchen giving her a slow, sexy smile. The door to her heart wouldn't quite close.

"You must be, Bea. Welcome," Stamos greeted.

The older woman smiled. "Mister Walker, you have a fine house and a fine family."

Stamos didn't correct her. Joy waited for his denial that she was a part of his family, but it didn't come. He gave her a happy smile instead. She didn't know what it meant. Smiles were not her specialty.

*****

Joy didn't know what to think, but she'd had enough of Stamos' smiles and overall happiness. The happiness that Bea added to the house was infectious, but Joy didn't think that Stamos' secret smiles had anything to do with Bea.

If he smiled at her one more time, she was going to pull his tongue out. That would stop his slow, sexy grin. He'd been so obvious that Bea started shooting Joy her own special smiles. Only Dillon's smiles seemed genuine.

The sun had set and darkness' shadows had come out. Joy raised her face to the heavens and sighed. It became a constant fear that each night in the free world, would be her last. Despite Stamos' promise, Joy still anticipated she could be imprisoned at any moment.

Joy heard his distinctive footsteps behind her. She didn't move, she still stood with her head tilted back looking at the night sky.

"Pleasant evening," Stamos commented.

"Yep."

"Joy, do you think you could look at me?"

Joy whipped her head around until her eyes met his. "Why? So you can smile at me?"

Stamos laughed a deep rolling laugh. "So that's it. I was wondering if you had a burr under your saddle."

"Bea's a fine woman," Joy stated, trying to change the conversation.

"She's a gem. I think that the wait was worth it. Dillon seems to adore her. I'm not fond of her calling him Dilly, but other than that I feel lucky to have her."

"I like her."

"Joy, do you like me?"

Joy's eyes narrowed at his honeyed voice. He was up to something.

"I had a meeting in town, as you know. You were the topic of conversation."

Joy gasped. "I already know what you have to tell me. I'm going back."

Stamos stepped forward and took her hand. "You're shaking. Joy, look at me. I found a way to keep you here at the ranch."

Joy studied him. He seemed earnest, concerned even. "All right I'll bite, what do I have to do?"

Stamos glanced away. He looked as though he searched for the right thing to say. Joy grew frightened as the silence lengthened.

"It's no big deal. It seems Bailey took exception to the fact that I asked her to leave. She called the parole board. They didn't know you were the only woman prisoner on the ranch and I guess it brought up a ton of ethical questions. They wanted you back tonight." Stamos took her into his arms. "It's quite simple really. Everyone agreed. Umm, you see..."

Joy broke away from him. "Spit it out cowboy. What's the catch?"

Stamos gave her one his slow sexy grins that she disliked. "It's easy, Joy. We get hitched and it all goes away."

"We have to get married?"

"Yep."

"Pull the other one."

Stamos looked puzzled.

"The other leg. Please, Stamos, don't fool with me," Joy pleaded, not believing for a minute that he told the truth.

"Joy, I'm serious. We are to be at the courthouse tomorrow morning for one of two things. Either we get married or you go back to prison."

Joy closed her eyes. This could not be happening. Going back to prison was not an option. He father had said she'd used seven of her nine lives. There was still a hit on her life, she just knew it. Slowly, she opened her eyes. "I want you to see something first."

"What do you need to show me? Just say yes," Stamos said, his impatience clear.

"I'll have to show you inside." She bit her lip.

Joy followed Stamos into the house and then to his office. She closed all the curtains and turned to face Stamos. She didn't want to see the horror on his face when he viewed her scars. He deserved to know. Slowly she raised her shirt up and over her head, standing before him in just her white bra.

She heard his sharp intake of breath. She didn't dare look at him. She already knew what she would see in his eyes, disgust.

"Joy, oh, Joy." Stamos moved closer to her. "How you must have suffered."

Joy looked into his compassionate eyes and nearly lost it. No one had given a damn about her suffering before.

"Prison?"

Joy nodded, her eyes misting. She tipped her head back to prevent the tears from falling, to no avail. "I have so many stab wounds. I'm not pretty, or pleasant to look at. Without my shirt, I'm the bride of Frankenstein."

"Oh, Joy. I have scars too. Two bullet wounds and I have a scar that runs the length of my abdomen."

Joy studied his face. Stamos was a complex man. "I don't know if I could be a good wife to you. You deserve more than what I could possibly give you."

Stamos moved closer and cupped her face with both of his hands. "We get along, Dillon is crazy about you, and I can't send you back to that place. Please, Joy, we'll work all that out later. Please just agree to be my wife."

Joy nodded and was instantly drawn into his embrace. Her tears stopped and she held on to Stamos for dear life. "We'll work it out."

*****

Joy stared at the ceiling, she stared at the wall, she paced, and finally she sat on the window ledge. The night seemed never-ending and at the same time, morning approached too quickly.

Marriage was something she had dreamt of, but it was a young girl's dream. Recent years had taught her not to hope for much. Stamos' kisses made her melt, but she knew that he would want more. A large part of her fear had ebbed since showing him her scars.

She wasn't a pretty sight, but Stamos didn't even flinch. Perhaps he never intended to see her that way again. She wanted to grab his offer and not let go. What happens after her parole was up? Would she be expected to leave?

So many unanswered questions and the sun began to make its presence known. A soft knock on her door made her hesitate, but in the end, she decided to open that door.

"Are you getting ready?" Stamos studied her face.

Joy turned her head away. "You still want to marry me?"

"Yes. Get dressed, we'll eat then go."

Joy watched him close the door as he left. There were no soft romantic words. Somehow, it hurt even though she knew the score.

*****

Stamos and Joy were on their way. Joy felt pensive. "It'll be fine, Joy." Stamos took her hand. "I know this isn't the way it should be. I should be bringing you flowers and taking you out dancing or something, but, honey, this is what we have."

"I know. I'm grateful, just, I don't know, it's all so fast. Will you expect me in your bed tonight?"

Stamos laughed. "Nervous and blunt. No, I'll leave that up to you."

Joy gave him a look of disbelief. "Really?"

Stamos parked the truck in front of the courthouse. "Joy, I want this to work out. We can make our own rules okay?"

Joy looked at him and looked some more. Finally, she nodded. "I'd like to make my own rules for a change."

The judge's chambers made Joy itch. Bad memories were all she had. There were a few people she didn't know, hell the only person she did know was Stamos. He'd been her rock during the unplanned fiasco.

Joy wanted to bemoan the fact that she wore jeans and a tee shirt, but she bucked up and pretended that it didn't bother her. She declined the plastic flowers the court clerk tried to hand to her.

A firecracker of a woman named Ida Perkins introduced herself as Joy's caseworker. She was from the parole board and she intended to make Joy her *special project*. Joy didn't appreciate the wording or the look on the old biddy's face. Ida had the look of a woman who went to the beauty salon and had her hair done. Joy had thought that the beehive look was out, but what did she know? Ida seemed to think it was the fashion.

Her heart tugged painfully as the ceremony commenced. There were no long looks of love, no secret smiles between them. Stamos looked handsome in his black western shirt and tight black jeans. Joy looked at him, but he didn't look back.

She knew what she'd signed on for, a way to stay out of prison. There were no promises of happiness. She knew the score. She always knew the score.

The ceremony ended with an awkward peck on the lips that Joy could have done without.

The door to the chamber flew open and a panting, red-faced Bailey stood in the doorway looking wide-eyed and panicked. "You married her?" she screeched. "You married a murderer? Oh my God. I never thought you'd marry someone so below you. She's the scum of the earth. She's a murderer."

Stamos stepped in front of Bailey and murmured to her. Joy watched as tears fell down the other woman's face. Bailey kept shaking her head in denial. Joy looked away when Stamos took Bailey into his arms.

"He didn't defend you," Ida Perkins needled.

Joy made no response.

"Took that beauty into his arms fast enough. Am I missing something? This is a real marriage isn't it?"

Joy took one long look at Ida and grasped her reason for being there. She wanted to prove that the marriage was a sham and send Joy back to prison.

"Of course it's real. Stamos and I will be very happy on his ranch."

"You didn't mention the child. What does your so called husband think about having you as the baby's mother?" Ida asked, maliciously.

"I married Joy because she is the perfect mother and she is the perfect mate for me." Stamos put his arms around Joy's waist. "I've already had one disastrous marriage. This one is permanent."

Joy wanted to smirk at the way Stamos practically growled at the nosey woman. It did surprise her that Stamos had been married before.

Stamos didn't put off Ida. In fact, she stepped closer to the couple. "I will be watching your every move. Have you ever heard how intense the INS can be about sham marriages to keep illegals in this country?" She waited for them both to nod. "Think of me as your own special agent, intent on proving that this is all a lie. Joy should be in prison. A murderer should never have gotten work release, but I am confident that she'll be back behind bars soon."

Stamos pulled Joy closer and kissed her cheek. "Bring it on lady. We have nothing to hide."

They both watched the brassy blond walk away. Joy started to shake, and Stamos embraced her. "Smile, we don't know the friendlies from the unfriendlies."

Joy nodded into his shoulder. "I know how to play act," she said as she laughed, pulled away from Stamos, and smiled into his eyes.

Stamos took her hand and held it tight. "I'll call George when we get home."

She must have let her emotions shine.

"Yes, home, Joy. Our home."

The warmth that flooded Joy's heart amazed her. "Well can we go home now?"

"Yeah let's blow this joint." He led her around the room toward the door, stopping to thank one person after another.

Joy focused on the door and to her great relief they walked out of it.

Driving up to the ranch house, they noticed a car that wasn't familiar. "Stamos, they're here to take me away."

Stamos parked the truck and took Joy's hand. "I won't let it happen. It's our wedding day, let's try to make it a good one."

Joy could tell he was worried. "A good day or good marriage?"

Stamos let go of her hand and opened the truck door. "Both."

Joy managed a slight smile. He didn't sound convincing. She climbed down from the massive pickup truck. This wasn't a time to get her feelings involved. She was fighting for her freedom. Looking toward the porch her heart dropped into her stomach. Ida Perkins stood there with her arms crossed. Taking a fortifying breath, Joy walked toward her. She'd survived six attempts on her life, she'd survive Ida too.

Stamos took Joy's hand and entwined his fingers with hers. She felt reassured that he was going to fight for her too. He was good, she had to give him that.

"Mrs. Perkins," Stamos greeted, tipping his hat to her. "I, well, we didn't expect to see you again so soon."

"I told you I'm here to check out this whole marriage. So far, I'm not impressed. No wedding cake? No presents?" Taking a step toward the couple, she narrowed her eyes. "I'm on to you."

Joy wanted to take a knife and cut off Ida's pointy snooty nose. "I'm sure that you can understand that the wedding had to be hurried along."

Ida smirked. "I knew it. It's a sham."

Joy panicked. "I'm pregnant."

She could feel Stamos stiffen at her side. She hoped he didn't look too surprised. "So you see, Mrs. Perkins, it is not a sham."

Ida sputtered, as she looked at them. Her face grew red. "It's Miss not Mrs. There is no Mr. Perkins."

Joy started to laugh, but Stamos elbowed her lightly in the side.

"Well, Miss Perkins, I think my pregnant bride has had enough excitement for one day." Stamos swept Joy up into his arms. "Could you open the door? I want to carry Joy over the threshold."

Red faced, Ida opened the door and closed her mouth.

Stamos still held Joy in his arms as they watched Ida stomp away. Slowly, he put her down and smiled. "Pregnant?" He laughed deeply. "Oh, Joy, how do you intend to pull that off?"

Joy felt stricken. "It just came out and stop laughing."

Stamos drew her into his arms and kissed her. A kiss he should have given her at the courthouse. "We'd better get on making you pregnant."

Joy pushed him away. "What?"

Stamos pulled her back against him. "There's only one way I know of to make a baby, darlin', and it isn't with clothes on."

Joy screeched as she pushed him away again. "Now just one minute, buster..." She noticed the laughter in his eyes. "I guess I really did it this time."

"Yep, I'd say so," Stamos said, still laughing.

"It's not funny."

"Okay."

"Stop laughing."

"All right."

Before she could say another word, Stamos kissed her on the cheek and walked right by her into the kitchen. He infuriated her, and she liked it. She loved the interaction with him. He was a contender and she respected that.

Walking into the kitchen, she found Bea in tears and Stamos trying to comfort her. "What happened?"

"Ida happened," Stamos said, in disgust. "She harassed poor Bea wanting to know all about us."

"I didn't tell that witch anything," Bea said tearfully.

"I'm sure you didn't." Joy scooped up Dillon and held him.

"She told me that I had to spy and report to her or I'd go to jail."

Joy kissed Dillon and held him close. "Stamos, maybe--"

"No, Joy, don't even go there. It'll be fine. Bea, why don't you go and lay down for the afternoon. Joy and I can handle things for a while."

Bea smiled. "I'm made of sterner stuff. My parents were Irish you know. I come from hardy stock and I refuse to let that mean woman ruin my day."

Joy leaned over and kissed Bea on the cheek. "I can see the Irish in you."

Bea gleamed. "I do have to warn you that she intends to give you a hard time and she expects you to sleep in the same bed."

Joy kept a smile plastered to her face. "It'll be fine," she said, looking at Stamos. He looked rather pleased and Joy had an overwhelming desire to kick him.

"Here, give me that little darling. It's time for his nap," Bea said, her arms outstretched to take Dillon from Joy.

Joy kissed him on the cheek. "Have a good nap, Dillon," she murmured.

Dillon chanted, "Ma Ma, Ma Ma."

Smiling, Joy turned toward Stamos. She was taken aback that he glared at her. "Stamos?"

"I need to talk to you in my study," he said in a clipped voice as he walked to his office.

Joy followed, confused as to how he could have changed his demeanor so quickly. She entered his office and closed the door behind her. Stamos looked out the window, ignoring her. It made her nervous.

"Well?" he asked turning toward her, still glaring.

"Well what? Look, Stamos, I don't understand."

"Are you already pregnant and if so do you even know who the father is?" he growled.

Joy took a step back feeling his words as a physical slap. Shaking her head, she stared at him. "What?"

"Oh come on, Joy, we both know what goes on in prison. There is no shortage of men on my ranch either."

Joy put her hand over her frantically beating heart. Stunned, she didn't answer him.

"Just tell me the truth damn it," Stamos yelled.

"Truth?" she asked boldly, taking a giant step toward him. "You want the truth? You stand there and call me a whore?" she asked, tears filling her eyes. "I... You..." Tears began to fall in earnest and she dashed them away with the back of her hand. "I'm a virgin you buffoon, and no I am not gay either."

"Really?"

Joy took a step back. She didn't want to be anywhere near him. She trusted him, liked him even, but not anymore. "Yes really, so you can go to hell. Why? Why would you ask me like that? Why?" Walking to the door, Joy stopped without turning around. "No one has ever given me the benefit of the doubt. No one had ever believed me or asked me my side. They always assume." She opened the door and slammed it behind her.

He was too dangerous for her. He had the power to bring her to her knees and she couldn't allow that to happen, ever. It had been as hard to stay alive, as it was to remain a virgin. Prison was a place of sex. Any and all kinds of sex. Disheartened, Joy walked toward the barn hoping to find a bit of peace with the horses.

A crowd of cowboys huddled around the bullpen and they didn't sound happy. Joy ran to where Bucko was kept. He was a giant, mean bull. Stamos was partial to the offspring he threw. Getting closer, Joy's breath stopped. Benji was inside of the pen and Bucko did not look happy.

Joy jumped the fence and jumped in front of Benji. "Walk backwards very slowly, Benji. Listen to me, do not run or Bucko will gore me."

Benji didn't answer, but Joy sensed the heat of his body move away slowly. The other cowboys began yelling and she shushed them. "Quiet, nobody says a word," she whispered, evenly.

Joy stared at Bucko. He glared back and began to snort. He tilted his head a bit and Joy imitated him as she murmured to him. Her body was soaked in perspiration. She was good with animals, but crazy bulls were something different. Not taking her eyes off Bucko, Joy took a slow step toward him. She heard the men gasp. She knew that if she retreated Bucko would be on her faster than she could run. She took another step. Bucko snorted again.

Joy could hear Stamos joining the crowd. He was being shushed. Another step forward and more sweet-talking. If he bolted, she was dead. Bucko tilted his head the other way and Joy copied him. His eyes grew curious instead of deadly. Joy knew she was safe, but she wasn't out of the pen yet.

Taking slow step after slow step she reached Bucko, talking to him the whole way. She lifted her hand and he smelled her. Then as though they'd been friends forever, Bucko rubbed his face against her body. It was hard to stay on her feet, but she did so.

Finally, Bucko walked Joy to the gate and allowed her to leave. As soon as she closed the gate, she collapsed into Stamos' waiting arms.

Chapter Seven

Joy allowed Stamos to sweep her up and carry her inside. It was such a foreign feeling, being in his strong, reassuring arms, a place to be safe. As soon as he set her on the couch, she put distance between them by moving further down the couch.

She took that moment to study her husband. His bronze skin and black hair made her think that perhaps he had Native American blood. His face awed her, so handsome with honed angular features. Joy looked into his dark eyes, flinching when she saw his fury. Hell, she should have played damsel in distress. He wouldn't be so mad, but that wasn't her.

"Just spit it out. Tell me what a fool I am, but I just want you to know that there was no way I was going to let that mangy bull of yours gore Benji."

Stamos stared at her, making her feel uncomfortable.

"You could have gotten gored yourself," he said, his voice rough.

"There was a moment when I thought that might happen, but it didn't. I don't cry over spilled milk."

His eyes widened as he looked at her. She felt similar to a two-headed calf.

"What? Just yell at me and be done with it."

"I'm waiting for my heart to slow. Damn it, Joy, you scared me to death."

Joy shook her head in denial. "It wouldn't have mattered anyway. Benji deserves a safe life. I couldn't stand by and see him hurt."

Letting out a huge breath, Stamos reached over and took her hand. "What you did was very brave. Joy, you deserve a safe life too."

Joy shook her head again.

"Joy, look at me. What you did in that pen was a miracle. You are a good and loyal friend. Don't discount yourself."

Joy turned and studied him. He appeared sincere. "I didn't mean to scare anyone. I just acted."

"Like I said, you are brave. Benji would be dead if not for you. I'm sorry about what I said earlier. I honestly don't know what got into me. I was cruel to you and I truly regret it. I know that you're as skittish as an unbroken filly. I feel it when we kiss. I know you haven't been with anyone else."

Joy gazed at him. No one ever apologized to her. Prison life she knew. This life, this life she was making with Stamos made her feel out of her element. "I don't know how to act anymore. In prison, it was simple. I kept my eyes open, my back to the wall, and my mouth shut.

Here there are feelings and niceties. Don't get me wrong, I love this ranch and the horses. I love Dillon, but as for the rest, I'm afraid that you'll have to show me."

Joy gaped at Stamos in fear. Maybe he didn't want the broken person she'd become for his wife. She was relieved when he drew her against him and gave her a quick hug.

"We can take it slow, no worries. Let's go see how Benji is."

Joy nodded against his shoulder. Relationships were overwhelming, but she became optimistic.

*****

Stamos took her hand in his, entwining his fingers through hers as he led her to the barn. He had a lot to make up for and he couldn't figure out where his anger had come from.

Joy kept turning her head, looking at him. She was probably waiting for him to explode again. She deserved his respect.

Benji looked fine, better than fine with all the men around him. The wide smile he beamed was new. Stamos hadn't ever seen Benji so happy before.

"Joy. Joy, you saved me." Benji hugged her, picking her up into the air.

"Hey, Benji," she said quietly.

"You saved me, Joy. I know now to never ever go into Bucko's pen again."

"How'd you manage to get into his pen in the first place?" Stamos asked. By the shuffling of feet, he had a good idea that it was some type of dare. A deadly one.

"Out with it. You guys look as guilty as seventeen-year-olds on their first panty raid," Joy said.

Panty raid? Stamos wanted to laugh but he kept a stern look on his face. "I want the truth. It's the only way we can trust each other and y'all know that we have to have watch other's back out on that range."

Again there were many feet shuffling, no one wanted to snitch. When Kid finally stepped forward, Stamos was surprised. Kid was a prankster, but up till now, it had all been harmless.

"I dared him to pet the bull," Kid said looking shame-faced. "I didn't think he'd actually do it."

Stamos nodded. These men had enough guilt that they carried around. "I appreciate you standing up with the truth, Kid. I know this goes without saying, but don't do it again."

"I'm sorry Benji, and Joy, I never meant for you to get involved," he said earnestly.

"I know," Joy said.

"You were amazing," Corny, the foreman, told Joy.

Everyone began talking at once, telling Joy that she was a hero. They called her special and the bull whisperer.

Joy laughed. "I'm just glad it turned out the way it did."

Rowdy pushed his way to the front of the pack, a toothpick hanging out of his mouth. "What's the punishment?"

Corny shook his head, but Arlo and Shep echoed Rowdy's question. They all looked at Stamos expectantly.

"A week of doing Benji's chores should do it," Stamos said.

Benji hooted in happiness.

"Oh and one more thing, Joy and I got married this morning," he announced, with a smile.

"I'm going to kiss the bride," Benji proclaimed.

"Be gentle and only on the cheek," Stamos instructed.

Stamos watched each man give Joy a quick kiss. He could tell that she was annoyed with him, but he couldn't help it. The look she gave him promised retribution, which was fine with him.

*****

Joy stood outside the door to the master bedroom. They'd both agreed that they needed to look as normally married as possible. They didn't want to put Bea into an impossible situation.

They left the rest of the sleeping arrangements the same, Dillon still slept in the master bedroom. Stamos enjoyed having him in his room, their room.

Joy almost turned around, but she heard Stamos crooning to his son. What could happen with a baby in the room? Plus she knew what Stamos thought about her. He might have apologized, but it didn't take the sting out of his words. He wouldn't be touching her, she was just another convict.

She tossed her braided hair off her shoulder so it hung down her back. Looking down at her flannel nightgown, she almost laughed. It was a gown of function, not of seduction. Taking a deep breath, she turned the doorknob and entered the room.

Stamos looked at her and smiled. The room seemed smaller with Stamos in it. He sat on the king sized bed holding Dillon, who was fussing. He had his shirt off and Joy had to keep herself from staring at his hard, chiseled, tanned chest.

Her insides quivered as she took in his big broad shoulders and his massive biceps. Joy's nipples tightened and tingled. Try as she might to pull her eyes away, she couldn't. He was enthralling. Sexy, very sexy, too sexy. Joy walked to the window and laid her forehead against the cool glass.

"Joy?"

"I'm fine," she replied, too confused to turn around. She never turned her back to anyone. Somehow, this had become a safe haven here with this sexy man. She straightened up and turned. "It's been a long time since I wore plaid. Stripes are my usual motif."

Stamos laughed a deep rolling laugh. "You are a hell of a woman, Joy." Looking at her, his expression sobered. "You have nothing to fear from me, Joy. I only want one thing -- well make that two. I want a kiss goodnight and a kiss good morning every day."

Joy's brow furrowed. What was his angle? "That's it?"

Stamos stood and put his sleeping son into his crib. He walked to Joy and put his arms around her. "That's it." He kissed her.

His lips were so lush, so pleasing. Joy jolted in surprise when he licked the seam of her lips with his warm, wet, tongue. Opening her mouth, his tongue entered her mouth. Instinctively she touched her tongue to his.

Emboldened by her pleasure, Joy darted her tongue in and out of his mouth. She wrapped her arms around his neck and pulled him closer. The moans she heard were hers. It embarrassed her for less than a second. It felt too good.

Finally she noticed Stamos pulling away from her. Heavy lidded, she looked at him in askance, wishing for the excitement to never end

"That was nice. Goodnight, Joy." He checked on Dillon and slid into the big bed. He noticeably occupied only the far end of his side.

Disappointment shot through Joy's body. He left her wanting. She shouldn't, she wouldn't complain. Sliding into her side of the bed, Joy tried to find sleep, but it was until the wee hours of dawn peeked through that she found slumber.

*****

Joy awoke with a jerk, sitting straight up. She'd learned to awaken ready to fight if need be. She noticed that both Dillon and Stamos were gone. The sun had just barely risen and already she was late.

She didn't want Stamos to think her a slacker just because they were married. Joy jumped into her jeans, yellow tee shirt, and boots, then scrambled down the stairs to start her day.

To her dismay, the kitchen was crowded. Ida Perkins, Bailey, Stamos, Bea, and Dillon were all staring at each other. It looked to be a standoff of some kind. Nobody looked happy except for Dillon, who caught sight of her and reached for her.

Joy ignored the adults, went to Dillon, and picked him up, sticky hands and all. He chanted, "Ma Ma," and continued to babble at her, telling her what had been going on.

"Here, let me have him, he's all sticky," Bea offered.

"I love him any way he is. I'll finish feeding him. We have a system don't we Dil?" Joy sat at the table and pulled Dillon's bowl and spoon toward her. Putting a bit of baby cereal on the spoon she bussed his cheek, making him giggle and when he almost stopped, Joy put the spoon in his mouth. Dillon happily ate and opened his mouth up for more.

"Well I'll be," Stamos said softly, watching Joy feed his son.

"She's such a good mama," Bea declared.

"If she was so devoted, then why wasn't she up earlier to feed him?" Bailey demanded.

Stamos looked right at Ida. "She was a might worn out from our wedding night. You understand don't you?"

Joy watched Ida blush beet red.

"No it's not true. There is no way he'd sleep with her," Bailey shouted, as she turned to Bea. She walked forward and grabbed the older woman's arm. "Tell the truth. They didn't even stay in the same room."

"Let her go," Stamos said, his voice deceptively calm. Joy could see the tick in his cheek and knew he was reining in his temper. "You are not to speak to Bea about anything. You are both to leave this lovely woman alone."

Bailey let go of Bea, her eyes spitting fire. "All she has to do is tell the truth," she challenged.

Bea stood straight and tall, as she looked Bailey in the eye. "I'm only going to say this once. They slept in the same bed. I will never divulge any other facts about my employers again."

"I want to see the sheets, I want proof," Bailey demanded then she laughed. "What am I thinking? She's a whore not a virgin."

Joy wanted to ignore her. She continued to smile at Dillon and feed him, but inside she raged.

Stamos walked over, took Bailey by the arm, and escorted her to the door. "That is my wife you are talking about. It would be good for you to remember that my family means the world to me. Don't come back," he said, pushing her out the door.

Ida Perkins looked shocked. "I'll be back, but not with that woman. I'm not getting answers with her here."

Joy watched Stamos close the door behind them. His eyes instantly sought her and he gave her an encouraging smile.

"Bea, I don't know what to say. I would understand if you want to quit," Stamos said.

"I've dealt with worse than those two witches. I'll stick with you."

Stamos kissed Bea on the cheek, causing Bea to blush. Then he sat next to Joy, putting his arm around her shoulder. "We'll be fine," he murmured, kissing the side of her neck, making her tingle.

Joy looked at him and smiled. "Can't get much worse."

"I'll be out in the barn." Stamos grabbed his hat and left.

"I'll take the little mister," Bea offered.

Joy looked at her. "I guess I feel confused as to what I'm supposed to do. I've never been married before." Taking a deep breath, she looked around. "Am I supposed to stay in the house or am I still supposed to work with the horses?"

Bea walked over to her and handed her a wet cloth. "I'd say that you need to clean off your little one and then skedaddle out to that barn and do what you do best, work with those horses."

Joy cleaned off Dillon, mixing in as many kisses as she could. Smiling, she looked at Bea. "Thanks for the advice."

"Any time, love. Now go get your man."

Joy surprised herself by giving Bea a kiss on the cheek. She never kissed anyone in gratitude before. All this craziness was making her soft. Walking toward the barn, she wondered if becoming a little bit soft wasn't a bad thing.

She entered the barn and to her delight Nanny, Nino, and Nanny's love, Pirate, were all in the birthing stall. A Billy goat was standing in front of it. "What the heck?"

Stamos walked over to her. "Nanny brought her entourage with her. I think you know everyone. Pirate is Callie's horse and Billy is from another ranch. I don't even know who he, I mean she, belongs to."

Joy stared into Nanny's eyes and laughed. "She's decided that she likes it here the best."

"Well in that case I'd better go and give Callie a call so she won't worry." He drew his cell phone out of his front pocket.

She heard a car drive up and wandered out of the barn to see who it was. To her horror two police cars drove up. Her father jumped out of one and pointed at her.

Joy began to back up, her mind whirling with escape routes.

"Hold it right there," one of the police officers shouted.

The beating of her heart roared through her ears. She stopped and put her hands up. She couldn't hear what they were saying, but she knew the drill. They were there for her and she knew that if her father was involved, it would be airtight. She was going back to prison.

All she could think about was Dillon. She wouldn't be able to say goodbye. She hoped to hell that Stamos would appear. She needed one more look of him, a picture of him to hold in her heart.

She'd known it would end this way. Somehow, she'd always known that she wouldn't be at the ranch for long. Her marriage would be annulled and as she drew a shaky breath, she knew she would be locked up in solitary once again.

Her heart twisted as she looked at her father's triumphant smile. Why? How? He seemed to take his greatest delight in seeing her suffer. She'd been a good and obedient daughter. The fact that he still had the ability to hurt her soul made her sick.

The cuffs were being placed on her wrists that she held behind her back. The officer began to pat her down. He seemed indifferent and Joy was glad. She'd had her share of perverts patting her down in the past.

Joy swallowed hard, refusing to cry. If it took everything she had, she would not let her father see her cry. The officer grabbed her upper arm, leading her to the squad car. Joy locked her gaze on her father and glared at him. The look he returned made her shiver. He didn't intend to let her out alive.

Tears pricked at the back of her eyes and she willed them away. A sign of weakness now would be a big mistake. Joy needed to hang tough.

She gazed across the hood of the black and white car and it crushed her that her father was smiling in glee. "Why?" she choked out.

His smile instantly faded, replaced with a menacing frown. "You know why," he growled, staring her down.

Joy didn't know why, but the need to know had a foremost place in her thoughts. It had agonized her every night since her initial arrest.

"Watch you head," the officer said, after she already banged it painfully. He continued to push her until she was in the back of the car.

Joy closed her eyes. Freedom and a normal life were all illusions. She'd known that all along, she just wanted it so badly that she had let her guard down.

The car started and Joy opened her eyes. Stamos wasn't in sight. He probably knew. It hurt that he hadn't told her.

"I thought I had a deal. Why are you taking me to jail?"

The officer laughed. "Honey, you're not going to prison. You're going to the Women's Psychiatric Facility."

Her heart beat out of her chest. "What are you talking about?"

"Your father had you placed there. You're going to crazy town. I think you'll enjoy being locked up with the criminally insane. From what I've heard, it's where you belong."

Joy looked out the side window. Fields of sunflowers flew by. Two dragonflies were mating. Joy stared as long as they were in sight knowing that she'd have only four walls for a view at the *facility*. Looney bin was a better word. She'd heard of the horrors of that place.

Taking a deep breath, she put on her game face. She got into her survival state of mind. The attempt on her life was likely to happen today. Her mind needed to be sharp and all thoughts of Stamos, Dillon, and the ranch had to be tucked away. If anything, she was physically stronger from ranch work. She had an advantage.

By the time they drove up the long, windy road to the huge monastery looking building, Joy was ready. Game on.

The building looked massive, all gray stone with moss growing on it. The gargoyles along the roofline made Joy shiver. They silently mocked her situation. Hell, if she were a gargoyle she'd be laughing at her too.

The officer held her left arm, pulling her along, up the stone steps.

Her father was on her other side, dancing his way to the top. She had to stay focused. It could be life ending if she allowed him to distract her.

The officer shoved her into a room and down into a chair, her hands still handcuffed behind her back. The nameplate on the desk said Dr. Hatter, Director. Joy thought he looked like a little weasel with beady eyes.

"Name?" he asked.

"Joy Walker," she said proudly.

"Just like I told you Doc. She's delusional. Her name is Joy Courtland. She thinks she's married and lives on a ranch with a husband and baby. None of it is true," her father professed.

Joy didn't say a word. It never helped. Somehow, her words backfired.

"You are her guardian?" Dr. Hatter asked.

"Yes, the prison released her into my care. She murdered her stepmother, my sainted wife."

Joy wanted to groan. He earned his title, King of Bullshit. How she wanted to strangle him. She knew that she had no power. She was at the mercy of the men in this room.

A brute of a man, a hospital attendant approached her with a needle in his hand. Joy began to struggle. The sharp prick of the needle was all she comprehended as her mind drifted. Her heart cracked as she thought about never seeing Dillon again. Her heart broke at the thought of never seeing Stamos again.

Loud voices jogged her out of her deep sleep. Stamos, she heard Stamos. Joy tried to move and to her dismay, she was strapped down, the ultimate imprisonment. Hadn't she had enough?

Turning her head, she spotted Stamos arguing with Dr. Hatter and her father. He was waving papers in their faces, but her father had his own papers. Being tied down panicked her and tears streamed down her face. Her father would win, he always did.

Looking at Stamos made her glow inside. He came for her. He came for her. He seemed tired and his hair looked as though he'd run his finger through it many times. His unshaven face gave him the ultimate, sexy look.

Joy's heart twisted as she gazed at Stamos. It'd been good while it lasted. They had a good friendship going. A good working relationship. He was the type of man who always had your back.

"I have papers signed by a judge," her father ranted.

"She is my wife," Stamos roared.

"Not in deed. Only on paper," her father said, smirking.

"What the hell does that mean?" Stamos asked, taking a step toward her father.

"She's still a damn virgin. That's what I mean."

"What the hell?" Stamos asked.

"I examined her. She's still intact," Wood said, looking triumphant.

Joy's cry of anguish went unnoticed by the three men.

"Mr. Courtland, that is improper and highly unlikely," Dr. Hatter chimed in.

"Truth is truth," Wood said.

"I believed you and your court documents, but now I can't go along with this," Dr. Hatter said. He walked across the room and pushed a red button on the wall. "Security will be here to escort you from the premises."

"You have no right. I'm her guardian," Wood screamed, taking a menacing step toward the doctor.

Stamos stepped in front of the doctor. Wood took another menacing step and he was just about to swing on Stamos when the security team came running in and quickly apprehended her stepfather.

"I'll be back," he shouted as the officer dragged him out of the building.

Stamos hurried to Joy's side. Tears ran down her face and she felt so helpless. "Untie her."

"Of course, Mr. Walker," Dr. Hatter said, unbuckling her wrist restraints.

Stamos took Joy into his arms. Sitting on the bed, he placed her on his lap, holding her while she cried.

Joy couldn't remember the last time anyone had comforted her. Despite knowing that she couldn't afford to become further entangled with Stamos, she stayed in his arms. Laying her head on his strong shoulder, she wished that her life had been different. After the initial shock of being imprisoned, Joy had accepted her life. Now she wished that she had fought harder. It probably wouldn't have made a difference. The evidence they had against her was damning.

He came for her. He came after her. He fought for her release. Her heart overflowed. She stiffened and stood up. She needed to put a cap on her heart. Pulling it out would hurt less, but she had to go into self-preservation mode and that did not include soft fuzzy feelings. It required cold, hard, calculating thinking.

A wave of regret washed over her as she looked at Stamos. He deserved better and when her three years were up, she'd leave, allowing him to find better. She looked at his outreached hand. She grabbed it and held fast as he led them out of the facility. Looney bin would be a better name.

"Thank you," she whispered softly as Stamos opened her car door.

Stamos turned her so that she was facing him. Framing her face with his hands, he leaned down and kissed her. It certainly wasn't a "you're welcome" kiss. It was a desire filled, soul aching kiss.

His whole body was hard and toned, but his lips were incredibly soft. His tongue, so warm and sexy, explored her mouth. Joy put her arms around his neck, pulled his head down, and pressed herself against him. He could make her forget everything with a single kiss.

She stiffened and then pushed him away. The separation was not only physical, but emotional too. She'd been melting in his arms one minute and putting up a wall between them the next. She couldn't seem to help herself from turning cold and aloof. Once again, she dove into self-preservation mode.

She hurt Stamos. His facial expression said it all. He looked bereft. One more burden to bear, it was all her fault. Prison mentality was too ingrained in her. She'd never make Stamos a good wife. At least not the type he deserved.

Chapter Eight

Joy looked at the empty bed. She'd slept in it before, but now it looked identical to an instrument of torture. Tonight was the night. It had to be done. Perspiration grew on her brow as she studied the object of her fear.

She'd received all kinds of smiles when Stamos brought her home. Bea fussed over her until she couldn't take it anymore. She mucked out the stalls with Benji. The physical labor helped with her anger. Trying to stay focused grew impossible, her mind kept wandering to her father and what he had said about examining her.

Her body shuddered and Joy tried to dig deep for strength. Every time she thought that she had a choice, it was taken from her. Now she had no choice. She had to lie under her husband and let him defile her. She'd heard one horror story after another about men and their rutting ways from the other prisoners.

Her hands shook as she pulled her nightgown off. It was this or prison. She flew into the bed and covered herself. Stamos said he'd be up soon. Dillon was sleeping in his own room tonight. It just added to her mortification that Bea knew what they were about to do.

The door opened and she squeezed her eyes shut. Joy listened to Stamos move about the room. The rustling of his clothes echoed in the room then the other side of the bed dipped under Stamos' weight.

Joy waited and waited, but nothing happened. Bravely, she opened her eyes. Stamos' stare caused her to jump out of the bed, bringing the sheet with her.

"Joy..."

"I don't think I can do this." Stamos was naked without the sheet. Her eyes honed in on his erection. "It's too big," she squeaked, backing away.

Stamos laughed. "Joy, I have no idea what is going on in that head of yours, but honey, I won't hurt you."

Joy shook her head in denial. She turned away. She couldn't look at him. From the size of him, it looked as though it would hurt plenty. "You won't have a choice," she whispered, her voice quavering.

Stamos got out of bed and pulled his jeans on. "Joy, what put that look of terror in your eyes?"

"I'm not naive you know. I have knowledge of what goes on behind closed doors."

Stamos stepped toward her. He stood as close to her as he could without touching her. "If prison is your teacher, then what you know is tainted. Making love is an intimate act that is pleasurable."

Joy stared at him. He looked so sincere. "I'll just lie there, you can do your business then we can be done with it."

Stamos sighed and stared at her. He took her into his arms and held her. "There will be no virginal sacrifice. When I make love to you, it will be full of wonder, passion, and pleasure. I can wait, Joy. We don't have to do this tonight."

Joy finally relaxed against Stamos. "But my father," she whispered.

"I'm not doing it tonight. He has no bearing on our lives. We choose. You and I." He stepped back and kissed her forehead. He located her gown and handed it to her. "Get some sleep."

"But..."

"I'll be back. I have some paperwork to go through."

Joy stood there long after he left, still grasping her gown in one hand and the sheet around her with the other. She didn't know what to think.

*****

An angel, that's what she resembled, a beautiful serene angel. Stamos drank in the sight of her completely relaxed for a change. This was the real Joy, the one without masks to hide her feelings. The one he wanted by his side always.

Realizing that he had to woo her, he felt lost. His ex-wife had chased him until he ended up marrying her. He didn't have to make the effort. Joy's reaction and feelings were natural. Her background tainted everything for her. Somehow, he needed to show her what marriage and trust were all about.

Ida Perkins would not ask for proof. It was barbaric and against the law. However, they did need to act comfortable and loving together. He wanted to be comfortable and loving with Joy. It surprised him, but he admired her. Most of all he wanted her. It hadn't been easy to get his jeans back on earlier. He wasn't one to cheat either. The wooing better go fast.

She didn't seem the flower type. She didn't seem the jewelry type either. He didn't have a clue how to court her. She loved Dillon so he had an in with her there.

Joy groaned in her sleep and Stamos pulled her into his arms. He didn't get his goodnight kiss and he'd be damned if he would go without. He pulled her closer and leaned over her, kissing her sweet soft lips. Her groan turned into a moan.

Stamos opened his eyes and found Joy's hazel eyes staring at him. Her sleepy look turned him on. She was a sexy woman. She had no idea that she looked beautiful. There were no pretenses with Joy.

Leaning in again, he kissed her deeply. She tasted of minty toothpaste and it made him smile. She must have felt his smile against her lips because she smiled back.

"Can't wait for my morning kiss," he said, as he settled her head on his shoulder.

"Me either," she said, with a great big sigh.

Stamos smiled long into the night, thinking of ways to woo his cowgirl wife.

*****

Joy woke alone, touching her fingers to her lips. There was no way that Stamos kissing her last night was a dream. She got up, showered and dressed, all in anticipation of her morning kiss. The kissing was nice, it was the rest that was bad.

Joy flew down the stairs and into the kitchen. To her immense disappointment, it was empty. How did she miss everyone? It was just past sun up.

She poured a cup of coffee and went to stand on the front porch. The day glistened with fresh dew and crisp fresh air. She used to dream of mornings similar to this. The steam from the coffee rose making her feel content. Drinking it, she embraced the day.

Walking into the barn Joy greeted Benji and Corny. They nodded at her with respect. It made her feel good. These were not men to give respect unless it'd been earned. They'd all lived hard lives too.

"Joy, could you give me a hand up here?" Stamos called out from the hayloft.

Joy scurried up the ladder wanting to get a look at her hunky husband. "Do you need me to help pile bales?"

Stamos walked toward her smiling. He looked like a hungry bull wanting his dinner. "No."

"No?" she squeaked. Her heart began to beat faster.

"I didn't get my good morning kiss," Stamos said lazily, pulling her into the circle of his arms.

"I didn't see you this morning," Joy replied, feeling butterflies in her stomach.

"Now you do." He leaned down, grazed her lips and pulled away.

"That's it?"

"What?"

Joy reached behind his head and pulled his head down. "This is what," she murmured, kissing him deeply, darting her tongue into his mouth.

The kiss lasted until Joy was sure she couldn't stand on her own two feet. Suddenly she let go and took a step back.

"Now that's what I call a morning kiss," she announced saucily.

"Yes, Ma'am. Do I get an afternoon kiss too?"

"Only if you're lucky." Joy scurried back down the ladder.

Walking outside to see the yearlings, she stopped in surprise. She just had flirted with a man. Hell, she'd been missing out.

Joy wanted to shout her happiness to the world. She settled on hugging Nanny and Nino instead. "You know what it's like don't you, Nanny? One minute I feel foolish and the next I feel bold."

Nanny's head bobbed up and down as did Nino's.

Joy's pleasure was short-lived as she watched Ida Perkin's car drive up to the ranch house. She quickly got out of her car, grabbed her briefcase, and seemed to be waiting for something.

That something turned out to be Joy's brother, Jamie. What was he doing with Ida Perkins? He was up to no good and she wasn't in the mood to have her happiness taken from her. Those moments were so few and far between that she wanted to cherish them for as long as possible.

"Joy, I think that you should come with me," Ida announced picking her way across the lawn in her ridiculously high heels. Her nose twitched at the smell of the horses and Joy enjoyed Ida's discomfort.

"I don't think so. You have nothing to do with me anymore. I'm a married woman and it's all on the up and up. Did my brother drag you out here with more of his lies?" she demanded narrowing her eyes at him.

"Don't be silly, Jamie has nothing to do with my visit. If you remember dear, I have the right to keep my eye on you. I owe it to the community and to the whole state of Texas to make sure you don't go crazy and kill anyone else."

"Well?" she asked, staring down her shiftless brother.

"Ida just gave me a ride. I met her in the diner and we hit it off."

Joy almost laughed as Ida blushed. Realizing that her jaw dropped open, she immediately snapped it closed. Whatever the angle, it didn't bode well for her. Jamie was using Ida. Joy tried to think of a way to get them off the ranch, but she didn't want to cause a scene.

"I thought I told you to stay away from here." Stamos put his arm around Joy's waist.

"Why didn't you call me, honey? I didn't realize we had company." Stamos kissed Joy's cheek.

"You can forget about the phony kisses. I know my sister and she ain't worth a kiss."

Stamos stiffened against Joy. She put her arm around his back and grabbed his back pocket. Stamos gave her a brief look and smiled.

"You haven't been around Joy since you helped to convict her. I don't think you are in any position to judge. For your information, Joy is a bright, loving woman that any man would be proud to have at their side. Lucky for me, I found her before anyone else had a chance."

Joy knew he was play acting, but his words made her beam with happiness. "Jamie, please respect my husband's wishes. He asked you to stay off his property."

The evil stare Jamie laid on Joy made her want to run and hide. "I thought now that we are all family it would be all right for me to come over for a friendly visit."

The fake smile on his face didn't fool Joy. "Well maybe someday in the future, but for now, Stamos and I are enjoying each other's company. Call first before you come."

Jamie stared hard at Stamos. It made Joy sick to her stomach. "Is that how it is? I'm not allowed to be here?"

"You heard my wife. Now back off."

"Oh dear, oh dear." Ida shuffled the folders she had taken out from her briefcase. "I don't care for this one bit. Family should treat each other with respect." She found a pad of paper and a pen. She began to write quickly.

"I believe in the same thing, Miss Perkins, but for now Joy is my responsibility and I don't want her brother around her."

Any happiness that had lingered from the morning vanished with the word responsibility. Joy had thought, she had hoped...

"I have a lot of questions, perhaps we can sit inside?" Ida suggested.

"Look, Ida, you brought Jamie here, you'll need to take him back. I won't talk to you with him on my property." Stamos walked forward, away from Joy.

It was a lonely feeling. The air suddenly chilled despite the wonderful sunshine. He walked forward without her. Her heart twisted. She had a bad feeling and she couldn't shake it off.

Joy stood there, watching Ida and Jamie drive off. Feeling at a loss, she walked toward the barn.

"Ready?" Stamos asked, leading out two horses.

"Where to?"

"I need to grab a few things in the house and then I'll be ready to go." Stamos handed the reins to her.

He didn't seem mad, what was he up to?

Stamos emerged from the house carrying his saddlebags.

"They are bulging. What have you got in there?"

"The kitchen sink of course." Stamos swung up into the saddle.

"I don't suppose you're going to tell me where we are going?"

"Nope."

His impish smile made Joy's heart begin to fill. Whatever he'd planned, he looked like he was expecting to have fun. Unsettled with the constant change of feelings, Joy urged her horse along and followed Stamos.

They rode next to each other most of the way. Joy admired that Stamos didn't try to take the lead. In fact, she admired too much about her husband. He had a great seat. He rode tall and proud and it was amazing to watch him in the saddle. In fact, the more she looked, the warmer she became.

The world opened up into a beautiful meadow, filled with tall Texas grass, golden rod, and a sea of sunflowers. The sky above was painted a darker hue of blue. The cool breeze caused the foliage to gently sway.

"Wow," Joy said, in awe.

"I know," Stamos replied, but he wasn't looking at the scene before him. He looked at Joy.

Her face grew warm. Joy dismounted and turned away from Stamos. She wanted to collect her thoughts, but he made it impossible. Her only thoughts were of him. His handsome face, his silky hair, his sexy dark eyes were in her thoughts. His big strong shoulders, his hard chest, his tight ass tortured her.

Stamos stepped behind her and pulled her back against him. They shared the beauty of Texas.

Joy felt content until she started growing warmer and warmer. "I need to get out of this jacket." She pulled away from him.

As she took off her jacket, she noticed Stamos taking a blanket and spreading it in the meadow. "What's all this?"

Stamos grinned at her. "It's a picnic of course."

"Why?"

Stamos sat on the blanket and started to unpack his saddlebags. He unpacked one plastic container after another. "Come join me," he invited.

Joy eyed him wearily. "That sure looks like a lot of food. Just when did you plan this?"

"This morning. It's a beautiful day and I thought you'd enjoy a picnic."

"I thought maybe you were angry about Jamie," Joy said, hesitantly.

"Joy, look at me. You have no control over the actions of others. I know it's hard not to think about it, but come here woman. I need to feed you." His tone changed from serious to teasing.

Joy nodded. She couldn't remember ever going on a picnic. She knew now she was helpless against Stamos. He always found a way to get around the wall she tried to build between them. She smiled and sat down next to him. "Thank you."

"For what, my sweet?"

"For this picnic, for being kind to me."

Stamos popped a grape into her mouth. "You make it easy to be nice to you, Joy. I happen to think you are a wonderful woman." He made a show of looking her body over. "A very sexy, desirable woman to boot. I won the rodeo by marrying you."

His smile was contagious and Joy soon found that she couldn't fight it anymore. Grabbing a grape, she popped it into Stamos' mouth. Her smile stopped as he held her hand and put her finger in his mouth. His warm soft lips surprised her. His tongue intrigued her. The sucking motion he made almost sent her over the edge.

Heat pooled in her lower region and her breasts became heavy.

Gasping, she looked into his eyes and what she viewed made her gasp louder. It looked reminiscent of raw desire, real desire for her. There was no leering involved. Her heart jumped and her body grew warm.

"Joy," he whispered, laying her down on the blanket.

"What?" she squeaked.

"Shhh. Don't talk." Stamos captured her mouth with his in a bold, passion filled kiss.

Joy opened her mouth to him. His warm tongue darted in and out of her mouth, making her feel a sense of excitement. Matching her tongue to his, she heard him moan. Stamos trailed kisses down her neck, causing her to shiver. She gasped as one hand made its way under her tee shirt and she froze, capturing his hand with hers.

"Don't. You already know how ugly my chest is," she pleaded as her eyelashes became spiked with tears.

Stamos stayed perfectly still, looking at her. "Oh, Joy, there is not one single part of you that is ugly."

"But my scars."

"Battle scars. You survived each knife wound. It's a blessing, Joy."

Taking a shaky breath, Joy nodded and let go of his hand. It surprised her that he didn't pull off her top. Stamos started kissing her again, stoking her passion.

Before she knew it, her top and bra were off. Looking at his face as he gazed at her chest floored her. The look of appreciation on his face was unsettling. It also made her feel beautiful for the first time in years.

"What?" she whimpered as he rubbed one hard nipple, then the other. "Ohhh," she cried, when he took one of her nipples into his mouth.

Arching up, Joy didn't want the pleasure to ever end. His mouth on her made her heart beat frantically. He lifted his head and Joy made a sigh of protest.

"We're just getting started," Stamos assured her with a sexy grin.

Taking off his shirt, Stamos gave her a knowing look. "Not bad for an old ex-lawman?"

"Not bad at all," she replied, huskily, reaching out to touch him. She ran her hands over his hard chest and pushed him onto his back. She kissed one bullet scar, then the other. She hurt for him as she traced his knife wound that ran the across his hard abs.

"Are my scars ugly to you?" Stamos asked.

"No not at all," Joy said, kissing his chest. She laughed as Stamos rolled and put her on her back.

He took off her jeans. She wanted it, she wanted him. She thought she'd burst if she didn't have him inside her. Just as hurriedly, she unbuttoned his pants.

Her body filled with flames of desire. "Stamos, hurry," she cried.

"Whoa, darlin, we'll get there." He kissed her inner thigh.

"No you don't understand I need you right now."

Stamos hovered over her, kissing her breasts again, he positioned himself between her legs. He reached down to be sure she was ready. He inched himself into her.

He was making her crazy with his slowness. Joy grabbed his waist and lunged upward, taking him to the hilt. "Oh," she said, feeling a sting of pain. Seeing the look of concern on his face Joy smiled. "I need you," she whispered.

Stamos drove into her, slowly at first, but Joy wasn't having it. She met him each time, taking him deeper and deeper. Feeling his body shake made her smile.

Suddenly she shivered out of control. "Stamos?" she cried as she convulsed around him. She was spiraling through the air with Stamos buried deep within her.

Joy heard him groan and shudder. His body spiraled too. The wonder of it astounded Joy.

"Are you all right?" Stamos asked, looking down into her eyes.

"Hell yea, can we do it again?"

Stamos laughed and held her tight. "Give me a minute and I'll see what I can do."

"Lay on your back," he said.

"We doing it again?" Joy asked hopefully.

"No, just lay on your back. Do you feel it?"

Joy closed her eyes and let the Texas breeze float over her bare skin. It caressed every part of her naked body. She'd never been so completely free. There were no brick walls, no wire fences, no bars. It went beyond the physical. There was no fear. Amazing, it was utterly amazing and she wanted to embrace the feeling. Tears poured down her face and into her hair.

"I feel it," she whispered. "Stamos, I feel it. I'm afraid that it will all disappear. I'm terrified that you and Dillon will disappear."

Stamos reached over and entwined his fingers with hers. "No one is taking this away. I'm not going anywhere and neither is Dillon. I know you have secrets. I have a pretty good idea why you won't talk about your conviction."

Joy tensed waiting for Stamos to say more. He just squeezed her hand instead.

"Are we going to do it again or not?" she asked.

Stamos laughed. "You are a greedy woman, Joy Walker," he teased. "Unfortunately we have to get back and I'm afraid if I give you another dose of *The Stamos* you won't be able to sit in your saddle."

"*The Stamos*?" she asked, laughing hard. "Maybe you're right, *The Stamos* is very powerful."

Stamos reached out, grabbed her, and pulled her on top of him. He kissed her deeply, almost senseless. "No one makes fun of *The Stamos*."

"I'll try to keep that in mind," she said, still laughing.

"We'd better get dressed." Stamos lifted her from him.

Joy liked the twinkle in his eyes. He looked adorable with his hair all mussed. The rest of him looked sexy. She looked him up and down and she smiled. "Well let's get *The Stamos* home."

Stamos stood up and grabbed his jeans. His whole body blushed.

"*The Stamos* doesn't look like it wants to go home."

"I meant *The Stamos* to mean my magnificent love making not a name for my... my..."

"Fine, I'll be good. Can we do it again tonight?"

"Woman, you'd better rest up for tonight."

*****

Bea gave her a knowing look when Joy brought all the extra food inside. Joy blushed. What was happening to her? She was a hardened criminal, wasn't she? She hadn't doubted that in years.

Dillon reached out his cubby arms babbling, "Ma Ma," to her. Happiness washed over her as she picked him up and held him. He smelled of innocence. Joy breathed in his scent. It was more than baby lotion and powder, it was the pureness that made her heart swell.

"I'll feed him," she said to Bea as she approached with a baby bottle.

"If you're sure?"

"Positive," Joy replied, settling Dillon into the crook of her arms and fed him the bottle. He was a little wonder. He looked so much like Stamos. They both had the same soulful dark eyes and black hair.

"You're going to be a heartbreaker when you grow up," Joy kidded.

"Just like his dear daddy."

Joy looked at the screen door. A woman about her age stood on the other side. She was a beauty with rich, shiny dark hair and sultry eyes. "I'm sorry? I guess we haven't met yet." Joy nodded for the woman to come inside.

Joy was fascinated by the other woman's curves. She looked perfect.

"I'm Dilly's mother, Stacey. Is my man around?"

Joy's heart skipped a beat. "Nice to meet you, Stacey. Stamos is probably out working with the horses."

"I've heard about you," Stacey said, walking around the living room, touching anything of value and examining it.

"My name is Joy."

"I told you I already know who and what you are. I came out here to make sure my son is being cared for in a proper fashion," Stacey said in a low warning voice.

"He's doing really well." Joy wondered what Stacey's game was.

"I will be the judge of that. I am his mother. Maybe I should just walk out of here with him."

"You'll have to speak to Stamos about that. You can't just take him."

Stacey smiled viciously at her. "I can do whatever I want. After all, we are talking about my son and my man."

Bea walked into the room and her eyes grew wide at Stacey's last statement. "Oh my, I'm going to get Stamos."

Joy watched her rushing from the room wishing she could take off after her. She didn't trust the woman standing before her smirking.

"I'm sure that Stamos will get this all figured out." Joy put Dillon against her shoulder and patted his back. He burped and Joy smiled.

"Did you want to hold your son?" Joy offered.

"No thank you. Isn't that your job?"

"Well not exactly..."

"Hello Stacey." Stamos didn't even try to hide his annoyance. His eyes narrowed and he frowned.

Stacey's face lit up at the sight of him. "You are still the sexiest cowboy alive," she said, rushing to his side.

She tried to hug Stamos, but he sidestepped her. "Why are you here?"

Joy grew disgusted watching Stacey's fake happiness turn into fake pouting.

"You know why I'm here."

Stamos shook his head and walked over to Joy. He sat on the couch next to her and took Dillon into his arms.

"We are so good together. I want us to be a family, babe."

Stamos laughed, causing Dillon to laugh too. Joy would have laughed, but she didn't know what the heck was going on.

"I'm married."

"To who? Oh no, not to this murderer. Bailey didn't mention that in her call. Hell no. Dillon goes with me. Right now."

Dillon started to cry and Bea rushed in to take him. "I'll put the little mister down for his nap."

Stamos nodded absently, handing Dillon over to Bea, never taking his eyes off Stacey. "Now you listen to me. You abandoned our son three months ago. I have a lawyer and I have full custody. You don't have a leg to stand on."

Stacey's eyes grew small. "I'll just get me a lawyer too. I'm sure once the judge hears that I'm in fear for the life of my little precious baby boy, you won't have a leg to stand on." She whirled around and stomped out of the house.

"Stamos..." Joy began to shake.

Stamos took her into his safe arms. "Don't worry about it, Joy. It won't happen."

Joy knew that although he tried to sound convincing he wasn't convinced himself.

*****

Stamos rode Frankie a bit harder than usual. He smiled wondering when he'd started to think of Franklin as Frankie. Stopping, he watched his cattle. Business was booming, it was his personal life that was out of control. Rubbing the back of his neck, Stamos took a deep breath. He never even saw it coming. How foolish, thinking that Stacey was out of their lives.

He was in no way as confident as he acted in front of Stacey and Joy. He didn't know what a judge would think. Hell, Joy was convicted of murdering her stepmother. That was as bad as it got. Trying to keep her safe might cost him his son.

He loved his land. Land that he had worked and built into a fine ranch. Everything was going to hell and he didn't know if he had the power to stop it. There was no way in hell he was going to give up his son. Stacey didn't even care for Dillon. Damn that Bailey anyway. From the sound of it, she had called Stacey and told her about Joy's background.

He knew losing Dillon would be devastating, but so would losing Joy. His heart hurt as though it was being squeezed in a vise. Dear God he loved them both. He couldn't wait for Stacey to get a lawyer. A judge just might give her custody. No, he had to prove Joy's innocence and he didn't care if she objected. They were in the fight of their lives and too bad if she didn't like it.

Stamos turned Frankie toward home and rode, not as hard this time. He needed to think of a way to approach the whole situation that wouldn't send Joy flying out the door.

Corny was outside the barn looking worried. Something wasn't sitting right with him.

Stamos jumped down, handed Frankie to Benji who also looked worried, and walked over to Corny. "What happened?"

"I take full responsibility, Boss. Somehow he got into the house and the next thing I know there was all kinds of hollerin'." Corny looked at Stamos then at the house.

"Don't act dumb as sand, tell me what the hell happened."

"It's Joy. Her father showed up and gave her a beatin'. I ran as soon as I heard the screaming."

Stamos took off running toward the house. In one sweeping look, he observed that Bea and Dillon were fine. Joy was sitting on the couch with a split lip and a black eye. Anger filled his being as he stomped over to her. "You let that bastard in here?"

Joy looked similar to a deer caught in headlights, her eyes big and round with fright. Tears poured down her face and she looked away from him.

Stamos swore as she tried to pull away from him. "I'm sorry. What the hell happened?" he asked, putting gentle hands on Joy's shoulders.

He wanted to pull her into his arms, but she winced in pain.

"It wasn't Joy's fault. I was in the kitchen when he came in. I should have stopped him, but he knocked me to the ground," Bea lamented.

"Are you hurt?"

"No, it seems that Joy took the brunt of that man's anger. He's an animal the way he grabbed her hair and slapped her face, yelling at her to keep her mouth shut."

"Could you put Dillon in his crib and then bring me supplies to tend to my wife?"

"Of course. I'm so sorry."

"Bea? It's not your fault. It's not Joy's fault either, and I'm sorry that I made it seem so."

Bea nodded to him. She scooped Dillon out of his playpen and walked up the stairs.

*****

"Sorry," Stamos murmured.

"It's not so bad," Joy replied, trying to stay strong. Any other time she'd been beat up, she hadn't had a choice. You don't cry in jail.

"Your face is swelling. I'll get some ice."

Joy laid her hand on his arm, stopping him. She liked his nearness. "Don't go."

"It's just to the kitchen."

"I know. Just sit here with me for a moment. I'll be fine, just give me a minute."

Stamos' concerned eyes almost made her tear up. Leaning over, she stoked the side of his face. His whiskered face tickled her fingers. This latest mishap just proved that she had to leave. Her heart was beginning to splinter. As she traced his strong jaw line with her fingers, Joy became washed in regret.

Stamos took her wandering hand in his. "Joy?"

"No, don't talk. I might come apart if you talk. Let me get my bearings, let me gather my strength."

"I'd kiss you right now, but that split lip looks painful."

Joy nodded. It wasn't the physical pain that hurt the most. She couldn't bear the emotional pain. It was her fault. She'd known from day one that she shouldn't let her guard down.

"I got here as soon as I could," said a large, older man.

"George. Oh, George, you should be in bed," Joy scolded.

"I'm fine, Joy, it's you I'm worried about. Hey, Stamos." He shook the other man's hand.

"Good to see you, George."

"Heard tell there's been a lot of trouble around my little gal."

Joy's heart warmed being called his little gal. She and George had been friends from day one. His job at the time was to escort her from the jail to court each day. When she was sentenced to prison, somehow George had come along. The long years in solitary confinement were only bearable because of George.

"We seem to have a situation. People are coming at her from all directions. Her father did this to her, Miss Perkins keeps threatening her, and my son's mother is screaming that she wants Dillon back."

George sat down looking directly at Joy. "It's time, sugar. You can't go back to prison. There are two inmates gunning for you and I don't think you'll live to tell about it. You need to tell the truth."

Joy shook her head. Her voice trembled. "My father and brother have both been here to warn me. They mean business. The only thing is for me to go back."

"No," both men shouted at once.

"Look Joy, I need you to listen to me. I'd rather fight those two bastards and put them where they belong. I can't protect you if you go back to prison," George said with authority.

Looking first at George then at Stamos, Joy nodded her head. She was frightened to the tips of her toes, but George was right. It was time.

Chapter Nine

"Let's go into my office." Stamos took Joy's hand, helping her stand.

Joy was glad for his strength. Her legs wobbled as she followed him into his office. It was truth time. It'd been so long that Joy wasn't sure what the truth was. It had become a bit muddied in her mind over the years. All except for the fact that she was innocent.

Looking around Stamos' office, Joy could see her whole life spread all over the room. Files, affidavits, and pictures, all as scattered as her life had become. It was sad that her life wasn't represented by a family portrait of happy faces. No, her life had all come down to accusations and judgments.

Bea stuck her head in. "Need anything?"

"How about a pot of coffee and some sandwiches?" Stamos asked.

Bea smiled, her eyes lingering on George. "Coming right up."

"Thanks, Bea."

The way Bea and George had looked at each other made Joy wish for things she couldn't have. Taking a deep breath, she gave Stamos and George a weak smile. "I don't know where to begin."

Stamos stood up and came around from the back of his desk. He sat on the couch next to her and took her hand. "The beginning, Joy, start at the beginning." His voice soothed her fears.

"My mother died when I was ten. Three years later, my father met a woman named Daisy. A pretty name, but she was in no way pretty. She was all glitz and glamour on the outside and pure meanness on the inside."

"Here's the coffee. I made sandwiches and my peach cobbler," Bea announced, walking into the room laden with a huge tray.

George jumped to his feet and took the heavy tray from her. "Here, a pretty gal like you don't need to be toiling so hard."

Bea blushed and smiled. "Thank you." She turned toward George, handing him the tray.

Joy wanted to giggle as they gazed at each other. At least it cut the tension around her. Her life may be crumbling, but she wished the best for her friends.

"I'll close the door on my way out and make sure you're not disturbed," she said, then hesitated. "I wanted you to know that Corny and Benji feel all kinds of sorry that they weren't here to stomp Joy's father into smithereens."

Stamos ran his hand over his face and sighed. "Bea, tell them I'll talk to them later. Just reassure them that it's not their fault."

Bea smiled and took one more glance at George. "I'll do that."

Joy waited for the door to close. "They were married for a little over a year. She was hell on wheels. Eyes in the back of her head. She knew every mistake I made and she would beat me. Daisy hated me, but Jaime could do no wrong. She was always hanging on him like a cheap suit. Jaime lapped up the attention at first. I only know what Jaime and my father told me. They said that Daisy was molesting Jaime."

"Did they tell you this before or after she died?" Stamos asked.

"After. I was asleep, they woke me up, Jamie and my father did. I could tell by the looks on their faces that something was horribly wrong. I could hear their hearts beating out of their chests. It was awful. They both had blood on their clothes."

Stamos took her hand in his and gave it a squeeze.

"They said that Daisy was dead and they were in big trouble. Jaime was almost eighteen at the time. They told me that if I said I did it, I'd only get a few months in juvie. Otherwise Jaime would get the electric chair."

"Here honey, drink some of this." George handed her a cup of coffee.

Joy took the mug and stared at it. Everything seemed so surreal. "They still hadn't told me what had happened. They just kept saying how family sticks together and how I had the power to save Jaime's life."

Joy closed her eyes. She could still see Daisy lying in the bed, her neck cut open. "There was so much blood. It was so red and the smell was overwhelming. I remember running into the bathroom and vomiting. My father, right behind me, repeating that Jaime would get the electric chair."

She opened her eyes and tried to wish away the images, but they were ever present. Joy swallowed hard, feeling a large lump in her throat. She stopped to sip her coffee. Stamos and George didn't say a word they just watched her.

"I loved my brother and my father. I was glad that Daisy was dead. She wouldn't be beating me anymore with her belt. They kept promising I'd get hardly any time because I had just turned fourteen years old. A few months in juvie compared to the electric chair. I chose to help my brother."

"Joy, you're shaking," Stamos said, putting his arm around her. "Do you need a break?"

How she wished he had asked if she wanted to stop all together. "I can keep going."

Taking a moment to regroup, Joy was silent. She felt so old, so very old. "We restaged the... it. They took showers, buried their clothes, and then they made me stand next to Daisy with the butcher knife. I had to dip the knife in her blood and shake the knife around so the blood would get on me. Then I intentionally put my bare feet in her blood and made bloody footprints leading into my bedroom. I was told to put the knife under the mattress and to get under the bed. They were going to call the police and I would be hiding under the bed."

"They alibi each other?" Stamos asked.

"Yes we made up a whole story on how it all happened. We went over it again and again until I could recite it all without thinking."

The anger radiating from Stamos made her uncomfortable. Putting her mug on the scarred oak coffee table, Joy squeezed Stamos' hand and let it go. She stood and walked over to the window. She wished she could enjoy the view of the horses at play, but her mind was filled with ugliness.

"They called the police. I hid under my small bed for a very long time. It was awful being covered in Daisy's blood, knowing that the police would think I did it. I kept telling myself that I was doing it for my family."

"Joy, come back and sit down," Stamos said, the worry in his voice went straight to her heart.

Turning, she gave him a half smile. "I'm fine here. The police arrived and they pulled me out. The light was on in my room, but they blinded me with their flashlights. It was terrifying to be put in handcuffs and taken away."

Joy paced for a moment, and then went back to the window. "I thought that was awful, but it wasn't the worst part. In fact, that was the easiest part of the whole ordeal. I knew my father and Jaime depended on me and I wasn't going to let them down. I was doing it for a cause. I had conviction in my actions.

My crime was so horrific that I stayed in the county jail until trial. 107 long days I sat waiting. I waited to be let free. They witnessed the bruises that Daisy had left on my body, I thought they'd let me out after they photographed them. I waited for my father to visit. He never came. He only answered one phone call I made to him. He wanted me to know that he hired a lawyer and to go with the plan. Everything would be just fine, but the lawyer thought we shouldn't talk until after the trial. It was a lie."

"Joy, why don't we take a break, sweetheart?" George asked, his voice so full of concern that Joy almost cried.

"No I need to get it all out. I need to be done with it."

George nodded to her.

"The trial was shocking. Besides my clothes and the knife, there was a massive amount of evidence against me. It was evidence that my father manufactured. Evidence he planted before Daisy was killed."

Tears rolled down her face. She thought she was past caring about it. Her father's betrayal still cut her to the core.

Stamos stood up and approached her. He opened his arms and she stepped into them. His embrace was her lifeline. She even shocked herself by how loud she sobbed.

Joy looked up when she heard the door close. George had given them some privacy. She fought to regain control of her emotions, but she failed. Stamos' shirt was soaked under her cheek. He handed her a clean bandana and his kindness made her cry harder.

All of her life she had secretly craved to be comforted the way Stamos comforted her now. It felt as wonderful as she always imagined. She took a deep breath, stopping her tears. As she clung to Stamos, she relished the feeling of safeness he gave her. It was fleeting, she understood that, but she was reluctant to let go.

Hearing the door open, Joy slowly drew away from Stamos. The look of concern in his dark eyes almost made cry again, but she needed to stand strong.

"I can go on." She gave Stamos a tight smile.

She chilled at the loss of his arms around her. For a moment in time, she imagined she was safe, but that was not her reality.

"Let's get to the evidence, that's how we'll try to prove your innocence," Stamos told her, his face full of understanding.

She clasped her hands to still their shaking. Joy walked over to the window again. It was easier than looking at Stamos and George. "Let's see, the first piece of evidence was an insurance policy I supposedly took out in Daisy's name for one million dollars. I was the beneficiary. That's when I figured out that I'd been set up. The policy had been signed six months before her death. In Texas, they call that premeditation. A passport with my name suddenly appeared along with a plane ticket to Argentina."

Joy looked at the two men and laughed, a brief, bitter laugh. "Why would I go there? Personally, I'd pick some tropical island. Then there were the supposed text messages I sent to Jaime in which I texted that I was going to kill Daisy. I didn't have a cell phone."

Joy sat down on the couch next to Stamos. "This is my personal favorite. I was supposedly poisoning her with arsenic that they found in my closet. The arsenic was to kill her so I could collect on the insurance. The prosecutor said that Daisy's latest beating escalated the whole matter and I slit her throat instead."

Joy reached a shaking hand out to Stamos and was relieved that he took it in his. "I was tried as an adult and sent to prison at the age of fourteen."

"Tell me about your lawyer," Stamos urged.

"He never met with me. My father was paying him. The defense he laid out was self-defense. I was so stupid. I didn't know that I could fire him."

"Damn, they piled you under fake evidence," Stamos said, his outrage warming her heart.

"I did my part too. I had her blood on me, the bloody knife, and the footsteps leaving the crime scene."

"Why? Why did they do this?" Stamos asked.

"For the money. There was a second insurance policy that my father took out on Daisy when they married. It was worth two million."

Stamos took a deep breath. "What I don't understand is how they were so sure that you'd keep quiet."

"I can answer that one for you, Stamos," George interjected. "They paid people to kill Joy. Luckily, she's still alive."

Joy sent George a grateful smile. "Thanks to you, George."

"What about the other evidenced they found on the computer?"

Joy wanted to laugh. It was all so insane. "I never even used that computer. They have texts and emails I sent to Jaime about how I'd love to kill Daisy. There were also some searches on poisons and the topper was the order for the arsenic. It was well planned."

"I'm so sorry, Joy." Stamos' voice sounded heavy with emotion.

"Me too," she said. "I just wish I hadn't brought all my troubles to your door."

"We'll figure it out together."

"I'm in," George said, getting out of his chair and kissing Joy on the top of her head. "I always wished that I could help, but no one would listen."

"We'll have to be careful. Wood and Jaime seem out for blood," Stamos warned.

"They've been damn smart and damn lucky so far," George commented. "Listen, Joy looks wiped out. I'm going to take off. I have to check on the rest of the guys out here. They are all my cases. If I made things worse by finagling Joy's work release, I'm sorrier than I can say."

"George, you brought a rare treasure into my life, so no you didn't do anything wrong. We have a lot of thinking to do. I want to find a way to expose Wood and Jaime."

"Take care of my little gal." George put on his tan Stetson.

"I promise." Stamos stood up and shook the older man's hand.

"I'll be by tomorrow."

"Thank you, George," Joy said, her smile wobbly.

George nodded and left. They heard him murmuring to Bea.

"I think romance is in the air," Stamos teased.

"It's about time."

"You care a lot about him don't you?"

"He's been all the family I'd had until you and Dillon. George was my lifeline, my sanity, my protector. I was only attacked when he was off duty."

Stamos reached out and pulled Joy onto his lap. Kissing her cheek, he then tucked her head under his chin and held her tight. "I'm here now."

Joy put her arms around him. "I know and I thank you."

"No thanks needed when love is involved," Stamos whispered.

Joy didn't know what to do. She never anticipated hearing those words. She'd fallen in love with Stamos despite all her hard work to keep her heart walled off.

She turned and straddled him, trying to get as close as humanly possible. Joy willed herself to just concentrate on the pleasure of Stamos. His hard body and his strong arms. The beat of his heart and the sound of his breathing. His scent drove her crazy, leather and freshness and something else she couldn't make out. Whatever it was, she loved it. It drew her as unyielding as a powerful magnet and she didn't want to let go.

Stamos rained kisses down the side of her cheek and down to her throat. Joy shivered in delight. She wished he'd make love to her and let her forget for a moment the colossal mess she was in.

"Joy, did you hear what I said? I love you."

"Y...yes I heard you. My whole being is glowing due to your words. I want to tell you how I feel, but I don't know how."

"It's hard, I know, but it feels good to say it," Stamos encouraged.

The silence filled the room. Joy knew what Stamos was waiting for. Her heart wanted her to shout it loud and clear, her head told her to pull away and walk away. She looked into Stamos' eyes, they were filled with love, desire, and hope. Feeling herself getting lost in his dark pools, Joy pulled away.

She jumped up and walked to the door, putting her hand on the handle. Taking a deep breath, she knew that this was one time she couldn't cut and run. Turning, she smiled at him. "I don't know how it happened, but I love you too, Stamos Walker. I love you with my whole being. It's probably the stupidest thing I've allowed to happen, but I can't deny it. I don't want to deny it. I love you."

Stamos seemed frozen in time. He neither moved nor talked. Joy was all kinds of nervous. Hell, she didn't know anything about this relationship stuff. She wasn't any good at it. Her heart wrenched as she stared at him.

Joy's eyes widened when Stamos strode toward her and picked her up in his arms.

"If you weren't sporting a spit lip, I'd kiss you senseless," he said, smiling into her eyes.

"I already feel senseless. It's foolish to proclaim our love now. Any moment could be our last together."

"Let's not worry about that today." Stamos put Joy down and kissed her on the cheek. "I have to go talk to Corny and Benji. I don't want them to feel bad about what happened."

Joy nodded. "I want to spend time with Dillon."

"You really do love that little scamp."

"I love you both," she said shyly.

Stamos gave her another kiss on her cheek and let her go.

Joy watched him walk away. He was nice to look at walking away. Hugging herself, she relished in what just happened. Stamos loves her. Who would have thought?

*****

After bundling Dillon up, Joy carried him outside for some fresh air. She wanted to check on the horses and she knew Dillon would enjoy it. She craved to see Stamos. She needed to look into his eyes to see if he meant what he said. Love wasn't something to take lightly.

Nervously, she adjusted Dillon in her arms and walked into the barn, enjoying the smell of fresh hay. She stopped at Frankie's stall and Dillon waved his hands, babbling to the horse. Love filled her entire being as she watched the interaction.

She heard Stamos walk up behind them. "He's definitely your baby. Look how he likes horses."

Stamos' arm snaked around her waist pulling her close. "Our baby."

Giving him a wary smile, Joy shook her head. "He has a mother. I'm just the stepmother."

Stamos kissed her cheek. "Nothing wrong with being a stepmother. You love him and he's wild about you. I notice how he always reaches for you and calls you Ma Ma."

"You make me feel all tingly inside," she whispered huskily.

"Good," Stamos said chuckling. "I've accomplished what I planned for today."

"What's that?"

"Making you tingle. Later I want to make your whole body sing."

"You do?"

Stamos laughed. "Don't look so surprised. I enjoyed being with you, making love to you."

Joy pretended that her whole body was not turning bright pink. "Yes it was fine."

"Just fine?" he asked incredulously. "Honey it was much better than fine."

"Where are Corny and Benji? They don't still think it's their fault do they?"

"I sent them on a fishing trip out at bootlegger's pond. I figured I'd give them a break. They sure do care about you. I want to show you something."

"What?"

"You'll see. It's important."

Joy followed Stamos to a wall near the front entrance to the barn. "You and most of the men aren't supposed to have firearms. Corny has finished his work release and parole. Both he and Arlo are done with all that. I have rifles stashed in case of trouble."

Stamos slid a panel on the wall and four rifles were stored there along with ammunition. Closing the panel, he told her to follow him. He hit the side of the ladder leading up into the hayloft, a hidden compartment opened and a rifle was hidden inside. "This one is already loaded. I also have two more in the hayloft on the west wall."

"But why?"

"I figured you may have to defend yourself at some point. I just wanted you to know that there was protection available."

"I know how to use a rifle," she said.

"Good. Just don't tell anyone about the rifles. I don't want to jeopardize the program."

"Of course I'll keep it a secret. I do feel better knowing they are there."

*****

Stamos yawned as he ran his fingers through his thick black hair. He'd been studying the evidence for the past few hours and it made him angrier by the minute. How he'd love to smash both Wood and Jaime in the face. They were monsters. How in the world could they have killed one member of their family, then set up and put a hit on Joy?

The evidence, the initial crime scene evidence pointed away from Joy. Whoever slit Daisy's throat was left handed. Joy was right handed. Blood evidence alone should have made the investigators suspicious. Wood handed them a case tied up with a pretty bow and law enforcement ran with it.

He'd been in prison during an undercover operation. It had been hell on earth. He was a big, fit guy, trained to fight, but going up against the prisoners was a nightmare. He couldn't even imagine what it must have been like for a fourteen-year-old girl to be thrown into that type of cage. Stamos' chest became heavy thinking about it.

The door slowly opened and there stood his wife. She wore a flannel nightgown, intended for warmth, not sexiness, but somehow she made it look sexy as hell. Joy's smile was hesitant and Stamos' heart squeezed. He'd left her alone all night. Of course she'd be hesitant.

"Hell of a day. I was just thinking about you," he said raising his eyebrows up and down.

Joy smiled. God how he loved that smile.

"Why don't you come here and I'll tell you what I was thinking?" he suggested with a smile.

Joy looked pleased as she crossed the room to where Stamos sat behind his desk. "I thought maybe you were disgusted with me and the whole situation. I waited and waited for my goodnight kiss and you never came."

Stamos pulled her down onto his lap. "Baby, I'm sorry. I'm a jackass for letting you worry."

"I wasn't sure—"

Stamos cut her off with a sweeping kiss.

"Ouch."

"Oh damn, your lip. I'm sorry, Joy." He kissed her cheek and made his way down her neck she tasted like sensual candy. She tasted so sweet. Stamos experienced ecstasy as she wrapped her arms around his neck and started to breathe heavier.

One by one, he unbuttoned the tiny pearl shaped buttons on the front of her gown. He exposed one plump, rosy breast and kissed it. He suckled her pebbled nipple until she squirmed. He exposed the other, toying it with his fingers as he continued to lavish the first breast with passion-filled kisses.

"Oh, Stamos." Joy sighed. "Oh it feels so good."

Stamos turned her so she straddled his lap, facing him. His heart quickened as Joy tore off his shirt and began to run her hands all over his chest. "You're making me crazy."

Joy smiled. "Am I being wicked enough?"

Stamos laughed and undid his pants. Pushing up her gown, he lifted her until she was in the exact position. He lowered her down and drove up at the same time.

Joy gasped and her eyes widened.

"Now this is what I call wicked," he growled.

Stamos loved her little sounds of pleasure she made as he lifted up into her, driving himself deeper. Her face glowed with passion. She stiffened, then convulsed around him. It drove him over the edge.

Joy put her head on his shoulder, panting. "That was one hell of a goodnight kiss," she murmured.

*****

Joy smiled at Stamos as he left to work with the horses. It had been an active night, both enchanting and wicked. Joy's smile disappeared as she thought back to the two of them in his office. It was grand at the time, but now Joy knew nothing but shame.

She'd seen that same thing in prison between prisoners and guards. Now it made her feel dirty. She reminded herself that Stamos loved her, but it didn't help. Remembering the tenderness he showed in bed last night didn't help either.

A knock at the kitchen door interrupted her musings. Her heart lifted as she greeted her friend and neighbor, Callie O'Neill.

"What? You're all alone?" Joy asked.

Callie laughed. "Garrett is pulling Daddy duty. I heard about some of your troubles and I decided to see how I can help."

Joy handed her a cup of coffee. "Might as well have a seat. I feel as if the weight of the world is on me."

Callie sat, frowning. "It helps to talk about it."

"Thanks Callie I appreciate it." Joy squirmed in her chair. She wanted to ask Callie about last night, but she didn't know how.

"I know about Stacey coming back. I'm sorry you two have to deal with her. Oh my goodness, I forgot to congratulate you." Callie immediately went and hugged Joy. "I'm so happy for you."

Joy wished she could be as happy as Callie. "Thanks."

Callie put her hands on her hips, studying Joy. "Out with it. Do I need to horsewhip that man of yours?"

Joy shook her head as Callie sat back down. "He's great. It's me. Can I ask you something? If it's too private let me know."

"Sure, Joy."

"We umm. Well Stamos and I were in his office. It was umm, well it was really nice, but now it makes me feel dirty," Joy said, trying to summon a semblance of a smile.

"It's not dirty, Joy. You are married and you need to talk to Stamos about it. I have a feeling he is the only one that can make you see it as a show of love."

Reaching across the table, Joy squeezed Callie's hand. "Thank you. I feel out of my element in almost everything around here."

Bea walked in holding Dillon, who twisted and tried to get to Joy. "Ma Ma, Ma Ma."

Joy took Dillon into her arms and he cooed at her. Happiness filled her being.

"You must be, Miss Callie. Happy I am to meet ya," Bea greeted.

"I'm as happy to meet you. I heard you are a wonder."

"Well it's a sin to brag." Bea laughed.

The atmosphere in the kitchen lightened considerably. Laughter and lighthearted banter ensued. Joy's mood improved by the time Callie left. She'd have to talk to Stamos about her feelings.

*****

"Did you have a good visit with Callie?" Stamos watched Joy walk across the yard to the corral.

"She's nice. She's the first female friend I've had in a long time. Of course there's Bea, but Callie is closer to my age."

Stamos watched Joy as she avoided looking at him. He couldn't imagine what could be the problem. "I forgot to give you a good morning kiss."

Joy still didn't look at him. In fact, she was doing a damn good job of ignoring him completely. He never did understand females, but this was downright puzzling. The last time, Joy was practically purring.

Stamos walked closer only to see her stiffen.

"Joy, is something wrong?"

Stamos expected her to look at him, but she just shook her head. Wrapping his arm around her waist, Stamos turned her around until she was standing right in front of him, facing him.

"Now I'm going to ask again, is something wrong?"

Joy looked at his chest and shook her head again.

Stamos put his finger under her chin and lifted her face toward him. Leaning down, he pressed his lips to hers. Her quick withdrawal startled him.

"Come, let's go to the south corral and see the foals. They are growing faster than weeds, eating me out of house and home," Stamos said, trying to lighten the mood.

"Fine," Joy said, absently. She followed Stamos instead of walking beside him.

Stamos stopped, turned, and threw his hat to the ground. "Damn it all, Joy. What the heck is going on? Why are you acting like I'm carrying the plague?"

Joy's eyes shimmered in the sun. She bit her lip and looked at the ground. Finally, she took a deep breath and looked at him. "I'm sorry," she whispered, her voice full of misery.

"Joy, just talk to me. Tell me what I did to make you so sad."

"I'm too ashamed. You must think the worst of me. I'm not a slut or a whore. Really I'm not."

"Whoa, Joy, where is this all coming from?"

"Last night we, I, you..."

"Last night? Joy, what are you talking about?"

Tears ran down her face and Stamos took her into his arms. He stroked her back and kissed the top of her head. "Joy, you are by no means a whore. Good God, you were a virgin until a few days ago."

"The women prisoners would ride the chair with the guards. They were the whores."

"Ride the chair?" Stamos asked. "I don't know... oh hell. Joy, did it upset you that we made love in my office?"

Joy nodded, her forehead leaning against his chest.

"Did I coerce you or exchange sex for a favor? Was cash given? No, it wasn't. Joy, I love you. What we do together is love. I never meant to make you feel shame."

Joy hiccupped and wrapped her arms around Stamos' waist. She looked up at him. "Could we try that good morning kiss again?"

"No."

"No? I don't understand."

"Let's work with the horses for a bit. I want you to get it all sorted out in your mind. When you're ready, kiss me," Stamos said, trying to sound gentle.

Joy nodded. "No one ever understood me the way you do."

Stamos smiled. "Good, let's keep it that way."

*****

Joy stood in the barn, buoyant wasn't how she ever thought she'd feel. She grabbed a few halters. She planned to kiss him later. His dark eyes had been filled with love and it was all for her. Her heart ached at the reality of it. If it seemed too good -- it wasn't usually good at all.

Joy worked side by side with Stamos as they led the foals with the lead rope. Something caught her eye at the far edge of the pasture, making her stomach lurch.

Dropping the reins, she dashed across the massive field to the fence. It hadn't been her imagination. Bridget, Joy's favorite filly, lay on the ground covered in blood. Her eyes were still open looking wild and distraught. Someone had tried to cover her with branches.

A knife lay next to the body. Bridget's neck had been slit. With one hand covering her mouth and the other holding her stomach, Joy walked a few steps and vomited.

The sound of Stamos running toward her gave her strength and comfort. Closing her eyes, she could feel the cool breeze whip through her loose hair. With a heavy heart, she opened her eyes and looked at Stamos.

Stamos walked to her, drew her into his brawny arms, and pulled her close, whispering words of comfort in her ear. He gave her a bottle of water to rinse her mouth.

Joy had expected accusations. It was a cruel warning to keep her mouth shut. She had brought danger to the ranch and the people she loved. It could have easily been a person laying there instead of Bridget.

She could see his anger. His mouth was set in a tight line.

"It's my entire fault. I never--"

"Shh, Joy. This isn't your fault," Stamos reassured her, pulling her back into his embrace.

Joy basked in his comfort, but she knew the score. Stamos didn't realize the danger they were all in. She'd have to go back to prison. She'd rather take the chance of being killed than have anyone's life risked here.

Lifted up on her toes, she reached for his clean-shaven face and pulled him down for his morning kiss. Little did he know that this was her kiss goodbye.

Deepening the kiss, Joy wanted it to go on forever. Balsam that was the scent that had been elusive to her. Stamos smelled of leather, horses, and balsam. At least she wouldn't have to wonder about it in her cell. Running her hands through his thick black hair, she relished the softness of it.

"Are you all right?" The look of concern in his eyes almost made her cry.

"I'm fine. I need to go into the house. I don't feel well."

Stamos gave her a sympathetic smile and nodded.

Walking away was life altering. Her heart began to break.

*****

Later that afternoon, Joy sat in the rocking chair in Dillon's room, holding him. He'd claimed a huge part of her heart and it ached. How was she going to let them both go? The die was cast. Upon coming home, after seeing Bridget dead, Joy had gone into Stamos' office to sit and think.

On his desk sat custody papers sent by Stacey. They looked damning. No matter what, Stacey was not going to allow Dillon to be in the same home as a murderer.

Joy couldn't blame her. She only had herself to blame. She never should have married Stamos. She was ruining his life. It was at that moment that Joy called Ida Perkins and told her that the marriage was a big scam and that the truth needed to be told.

Ida had sounded almost gleeful on the phone. She was coming before dusk with a deputy to escort her back to prison. In doing so, it gave Joy a certain amount of peace. It was the right thing to do. They'd all see and understand one day.

Maybe she could come back in three years. Her eyes misted as she looked at the child in her arms. He wouldn't remember her.

"Be good for your daddy. He's a good man and I love you both so much. I'm going to burst."

"Everything okay?" Stamos asked, staring at her.

Joy summoned a smile. "Just telling Dillon how much I love you both."

She could feel his scrutiny. She knew he sensed that something wasn't right. She couldn't tell him. It would be too hard. Joy planned to wait for Ida and the deputy to show up and take her away. She just hoped that Stamos wouldn't hate her for it.

The sun was setting. Joy put Dillon in his crib and gave him one last kiss on his head. Pain filled her being as she walked away. The doorbell rang and she hurried down the stairs. Stamos would understand in time. She only wanted to keep them safe.

She walked into the kitchen and flinched at Stamos' angry and accusing eyes. "What the hell, Joy?"

"Stamos, it's for the best," she said, imploring him to forgive her with her eyes.

"Joy, don't go," he pleaded.

"Too late for that, Mr. Walker." The deputy handcuffed Joy's hands behind her.

Ida smirked at Stamos. "I'm always right. This sham of a marriage stank to high heavens from the first."

Stamos' eyes clashed with Joy's. "A sham?"

Joy bit her bottom lips so hard that it started to bleed. "Yes a sham," she whispered, her throat feeling raw. "I'm sorry."

Joy walked out to the police car. She looked for one last glimpse of Stamos, but he didn't come out of the house. Her heart shattered. She knew she had just inflicted a hard blow to her husband.

Chapter Ten

Three long weeks, that's how long Joy had been in the SHU, the solitary housing unit. The four walls seemed to close in on her. It was worse coming back after experiencing the freedom of the ranch. Most of the time she shut down, emotions killed.

Her first week in prison ended in disaster. The long awaited attempt on her life finally came. By the time it finally happened, Joy was wound tight. Every move, every shadow caused her to jump.

While in line walking to the cafeteria, it happened. Sour Jane, the chosen assassin, almost earned her pay. She came charging up the line and lunged for Joy with a shank in her hand. Joy spotted it coming and bent her knees ready to attack.

Thank God, for Beefy Brenda, an old acquaintance whom Joy had defended once. She threw herself at Sour Jane, trying to blindside her. Beefy Brenda's massive weight knocked Sour Jane to the floor.

Joy ended up with a sliced arm, but it could have been fatal. She lay on the cold stone floor bleeding profusely, knowing that her father was not going to stop until she was dead. The guards hurried her to the infirmary and the doctor patched her up. Fifteen stiches without pain meds, she'd been through it before. She kept her mind blank the whole time. Thinking about Stamos and Dillon would have made it worse.

Every morning she remembered that she owed Stamos a good morning kiss and no matter how hard she tried to turn her heart to stone, she couldn't. Missing Stamos and Dillon was a constant, unbearable ache she carried in her heart. She had to push through. Missing them, needing them would be her death. The constant longing had to stop. Somehow, she'd have to forget them. This was her life, this prison cell, and she'd do best to remember that.

Every night she fought to stay strong. She lectured herself and willed herself to forget about the ranch. Four long, lonely weeks. That's how long it had been since she had seen a smile or heard a kind word. The new night guard had been giving her the eye and it petrified her. Around the SHU it was give in or else. The prisoners in her housing unit were considered expendable. She often heard screams in the middle of the night. Her turn would be soon enough. The fact that she was powerless destroyed her. She needed to buck up or she wouldn't survive.

Stamos and George came each visiting day, but she refused visitors. It would be too unbearable to see the love of her life and then have to go back to her cell. Especially since she was putting that life behind her.

It had all been a big mistake, one huge mistake, calling Ida Perkins.

Being in prison wouldn't keep her loved ones safe. She'd heard from the prison grapevine that there had been an abundance of accidents at the ranch. Her sacrifice had been for naught, once again.

Joy held Stamos' latest letter. He wrote everyday, but she never opened them. Emotionally she wasn't capable. She needed to stay strong and focused. Not only for her sake, but also for the sake of her unborn child.

Stamos deserved to know. He'd have to make plans to take their baby after it was born. A sob was buried deep in her chest, but she had to keep it in. It would be lights out soon and that guard Smalz would be on duty.

*****

Stamos stared sightlessly out his office window. He couldn't seem to stop his brooding. It had been visiting day at the prison and once again, he was turned away. A knife slashed his heart every time he heard the refusal. He still went. Maybe he was just plain crazy.

Joy made her choice. He knew that he should accept it, but he just couldn't. No matter what he did, she was on his mind. Everywhere he looked, he pictured her. He was reminded by each horse she had worked with and most of all he was reminded by Dillon. Who knew that little Dillon would even know she was gone, but he did.

Bea said he was teething, but when he cried, he cried for his Ma Ma. It broke Stamos' heart.

The other problem was Bailey. She showed up everywhere he went. Stacey withdrew her petition for custody and left town. Good riddance. Now if he could get rid of Bailey.

Pouring himself some whiskey, Stamos shook his head. Joy had been attacked her first day back. He knew she was being housed in the SHU and he didn't like it one bit. He downed the whiskey and slammed the glass down on his desk. Good God, what was he going to do?

He gave George a ghost of a smile as the older man entered the room. "Hey, George."

"I've got news. Joy wants to see you," he said, sounding worried.

Stamos sighed. "Why?"

"I don't rightly know. I just got the call. You can see her tomorrow. I thought I'd drive out to tell you in person."

"I appreciate it, George."

"I know," George said, as he left.

Stamos rubbed his hand over his weary face. It was probably more bad news. He hoped she wouldn't insist on a divorce. He couldn't bear it. His heart had been torn out and stomped on.

She wasn't safe. Hell, no one was safe. The amount of accidents around the ranch was no coincidence. Someone had dug holes in the back pastures causing Arlo to fall and break his arm. The horse he'd been riding, Desi, had to be put down. The barn had been set on fire. Fortunately only one wall was burned. Every day it was something else. He needed to catch them in the act.

*****

Stamos twirled the key ring around his finger. He couldn't sit still. He'd been waiting over an hour for the guards to call him. His stomach was tied in knots and his heart fluttered. What if she wanted a divorce? He could take anything, well almost. If she told him she didn't love him, he knew he'd crumble.

He wanted to pace but they told him to sit. He felt akin to a caged animal. He hated this place. Knowing how much Joy relished wide-open places, his heart grew heavy. She must be suffering in the SHU. Oh, God, he had to get her out. Somehow, he'd have to convince her to change her mind. Even then, he wasn't positive she could be released again.

They finally called him over, checked his ID, and patted him down. He had to leave his Stetson and personal effects with the guard, but Stamos didn't care. He just wanted a glimpse of his wife. He ached for the sight of her. He wanted to see her beautiful, expressive hazel eyes.

Why did she want to see him? Why now? He sat at the metal table with the chairs attached. It brought back bad memories of his undercover mission. Prison was hell, pure and simple. He watched as each woman walked into the visitor's room. The waiting tortured him.

She was a sight for his sore eyes. He'd missed her, heart and soul.

Joy gave him a tentative smile. "Hello, Stamos," she said quietly.

Stamos motioned for her to sit across from him. They were not to have contact. "I wish I could say you look good, but I can't lie. You look pale and tired."

Joy nodded. "I know. It's hard to sleep."

"Are you all right? The news that you were attacked scared me to death."

"I'm fine. It could have been worse," she said, studying his face.

Stamos knew that she was drinking in the sight of him, just as he was drinking in the sight of her. "Why did you refuse to see me?"

Joy looked as though she was about to cry. Biting her lip, she looked away. Finally, she looked at him. "Because saying goodbye to you would break me."

"Oh, Joy," Stamos said, sighing. "I understand, but you could have told me."

"I'm sorry."

"Are you being treated all right?"

"All in all, yes. If you could get a message to George about the night guard, I'd appreciate it. I feel so stupid. My father is cruel and vindictive.

I didn't know he'd go after you to get to me. I thought I was protecting you and Dillon," she said, her voice cracking.

"We need to get you out of here. Tell me about the guard, has he touched you?"

Joy shook her head. "No he hasn't, I just don't trust him. Just tell George that. As far as getting out of here, I doubt that will happen. Ida Perkins wants me to rot in this place for some reason."

"You're here because you said that our marriage is a sham," Stamos said, the hurt in his voice was evident to him.

"I'm so sorry. I love you," Joy professed.

Stamos' head snapped toward the door as the guard announced that visiting time was over. They'd barely had time to talk.

"I love you too."

They both stood staring at each other, the guard approaching. "I'm pregnant, Stamos. I need you to make plans to take the child after it's born."

Stamos stared at her as the guard ushered her out of the room. He needed to find a way to get her released immediately.

The ride home was miserable. Stamos drove on autopilot. Her news stunned him. A baby. He never -- oh hell who was he kidding, he should have known better. That's how Dillon was conceived. After that, he'd sworn he'd always practice safe sex.

As the news sank in, he was pleased. It wasn't the ideal time, but he wanted children with Joy. She'd looked scared. He'd have to find out who this night guard was and give him the devil. He still had contacts from his law enforcement days.

All of the men hustled out of the barn and waited for him to get out of the truck. Stamos sighed. It seemed to be one thing wrong after another.

"What's wrong?" Stamos asked Corny, who looked like he wanted to kill something.

"Some bastard shot five calves last night. The Kid and Arlo found the carcasses this morning. Shot through the head. Their mamas stayed nearby. It was the worst thing I'd seen in a long time. We herded the cows to a different pasture, one closer to the house."

"You did the right thing," Stamos assured the other man. "You all did."

"How's Joy?" Benji asked, his eyes brightening when he said her name.

"She'll be fine, she looks a bit tired."

"Did you tell her that I missed her?" Benji asked eagerly.

"Yep. She misses y'all too." Stamos looked at Corny. "Saddle up a few horses I want to see the damage."

"All ready have them ready. Knew you'd want to see them first thing."

Stamos nodded his thanks. Joy had been right. She'd gone back to prison for naught. Her damn family seemed determined to ruin his ranch. He had a bad feeling that this was just the beginning.

He'd go see the dead animals, and then he planned to find out who the night guard was. There was going to be hell to pay. He needed to call George and tell him about the guard and Joy's pregnancy. Joy's pregnancy, by God he just might have a way to get her out.

*****

Joy sat on her bunk, her knees drawn up with her arms around them. Sleep eluded her. The regular night guard wasn't on duty, but Joy still dreaded the evening. Something was going to happen, it was in the air.

She tried to make her worries go away, but it became impossible. The starkness of the cage she lived in added to her fears. Joy wished she'd had one personal item to hold or a picture to look at. She didn't have anything to draw comfort from, only her memory of Stamos' face.

He loved her. The way he looked at her confirmed it. She'd been so afraid that he'd hate her for leaving. Her life was a tangled mess.

It'd been that way ever since Daisy's death, Daisy's murder. It was hard to think about, but she had to for the sake of her marriage and for the sake of her children, Dillon and the one she carried.

Despondently, she wondered is Dillon missed her. He was probably too young she concluded. The night was long, and lonely. Her thoughts didn't help pass the time, they were torturous.

Finally, the light came on, indicating that it was morning. She'd survived another night. Sighing in relief, she stepped to the cell bars, looking to see who the new guard was. To her horror, it was Smalz, the guard from hell. Joy gasped as she caught sight of him, but schooled her face to show no emotion as he leered at her.

"Morning slut," Smalz greeted as he looked her up and down. He started to walk away, but he turned back. "I have plans for you today."

Hell, she was in hell, with no way to escape. Joy knew what that look meant. He was pulled off night duty and he wasn't happy. She would pay. She'd have to watch her back. Fear for her baby consumed her. Taking a deep breath, she put on her prison persona, cold, hard, and uncaring.

Joy waited, and waited. It was a day of expecting Smalz to make his move, and make a move she was positive he would. She declined her shower, which killed her since she looked forward to the hot water cleansing her.

Being in the SHU, she ate all her meals in her cell. Besides shower time, which was twice a week, she had daily exercise time. One hour in an outdoor chain link cage, weather permitting. All she had to read was a Bible. She'd become familiar with it once again.

Joy'd been on edge all day. Lunch was served, a cheese sandwich and an apple. It was her scheduled time for exercise, but Smalz didn't show up to get her. Not knowing what to think, she grew anxious. Something was up.

It wasn't a surprise when her cell door opened and Smalz let himself in, closing the door behind him. Joy scrambled to the farthest corner of her bunk, panicking.

"Thought you could interfere in my life and not have any consequences? Think again you whore," Smalz said as his bloated face grew red. His huge belly strained the buttons of his uniform. She prayed his girth would make him unwieldy.

"I'm not worth it, Smalz. Don't ruin your career over me. I didn't have anything to do with your schedule change," Joy said, deceivingly calm.

The look in his eyes dried up all hope. He was going to extract his revenge and he was going to do it now. Joy got to her feet so she could try to dodge him. She jumped one way then another avoiding his beefy hands.

Her luck didn't hold. Smalz grabbed her hair and backhanded her face. She could feel her cheek slice open as his ring gouged her. He slapped her again, throwing her to the ground. In desperation, Joy wrapped her arms over her head as the crushing force of his baton hit her shoulders. She bit her tongue to keep from screaming. She wouldn't give him the satisfaction.

"On your knees, whore. You have to make this all up to me, today and every day," he shouted, unbuckling his belt.

Joy prayed as she heard his zipper unzip. This was it. She had feared this very thing for eight long years. His hands in her hair pulled her toward him. She had never experienced such pain. Looking at him, she almost vomited. The smell of him was worse.

He hit her on the back with his baton, demanding that she open her mouth. She refused. He raised his arm again and Joy thought he would kill her this time.

"Smalz, don't you touch her," a female guard warned, as she got on the radio and called for help.

Smalz threw her on the bed and zipped himself up. "You'd better keep your mouth shut," he warned. "Seems like your good at it."

Joy watched Smalz leave her cell. No one came in to help her. No one asked if she was hurt. Somehow, it didn't surprise her.

*****

Waking, Joy could feel the pain of her body. She'd often heard the phrase, *feels like I've been hit by a truck,* now she knew the true meaning.

She immediately recognized that she wasn't in the prison infirmary, she was in the hospital. She reached down and held her abdomen. She figured there was only one reason she was there, she must have lost the baby.

No matter how much she tried to deny it, she couldn't. She had been born under a cursed star. Everything she touched became cursed too. Joy waited in vain for the tears to start. They never materialized. An overwhelming feeling of hollowness filled her being.

She was alone. It was as it should be, she reasoned. Everyone she touched came to harm. The dangers of prison frightened her. Smalz would be out for blood. She knew the score, they'd blame her for the whole incident. She prayed that they didn't add more time to her sentence. It didn't matter, not anymore.

They hadn't handcuffed her to the bed. She must be injured worse than she fathomed. The prison officials didn't seem to think she'd escape.

Joy held her breath when the door opened. She released it as Stamos walked into the room. He looked so tired with bags under his eyes and he hadn't shaved. His black hair looked tousled as though he'd run his finger through it a million times. Her heart went out to him. The loss of the baby was his loss too.

Watching as he closed the gap between them, Joy tried to feel something. Perhaps she was in shock. That would explain her hollow feeling. "You're here."

Stamos sat on the side of the bed and took Joy's hand in his. He gave her a ghost of a smile. "I'm glad you're finally awake."

"You don't have to try to be cheerful on my account. I already know." Joy tried to keep her voice even.

"The warden was here already? I wanted to tell you."

Joy shook her head. "The warden? No he hasn't been here."

Stamos looked puzzled. "Then who told you?"

"I just know. I feel so bad for you. I know you had plans. It'll make divorcing me easier."

"Wait a minute. Let's back up. What do you already know?"

"The baby is gone. Why else would I be in the hospital?"

"Joy, you didn't lose the baby. The baby is fine," he said, tucking a piece of hair behind her ear.

"Then why am I here? I should be in the prison infirmary. My injuries can't be that bad are they?"

"No you're bruised and there is a bandage on your cheek, but you'll be fine."

"I still don't understand."

Stamos smiled at her. "You are going home with me. The doctor said you could go home and your home is with me," he said, stoking her hand.

"I don't understand. How?"

"Well, I had a little chat with Ida Perkins. Your pregnancy negated your claim that our marriage is a sham. It seems that Ida knows your family pretty darn well. I was able to trace money exchanging hands. Your father paid her well."

Joy blinked and looked down at their entwined hands. It wasn't possible that she was going back to the ranch. She was afraid to move, she was afraid to think. It had to be wrong.

"Why are you saying such things? I know I'm going back to prison," Joy said, her voice getting a bit hysterical.

"Whoa, Joy. Just breathe for a minute. It's true. I know you've been through a rough time, but sweetheart you've got to believe me."

Joy blinked and looked up at Stamos. She saw the truth in his eyes and sagged against the pillow whispering, "Thank God. Thank God."

The door opened and Bea walked in with little Dillon in her arms. She smiled as she approached the bed. "Glad I am to see ya, Joy. This little one hasn't stopped frettin' since you've been gone."

"Ma Ma, Ma Ma, Ma Ma," Dillon chanted, reaching out for Joy. She opened her arms and held him close. She needed to touch every part of him to reassure herself that he was all right.

"I love you, Dillon," she whispered, holding him against her shoulder.

"Can't wait to get you home and fed proper-like. You look skinny," Bea said.

Joy witnessed the look of concern that Stamos and Bea exchanged.

"Your fine cooking will fix her right up," Stamos said.

Joy smiled at them. "It's like a dream. I still can't believe I'm going home."

"Believe it, darlin', believe it."

*****

Joy walked to the edge of the yard, looking out at the waking day. The sun was rising with its orange and yellow glory. The coolness in the air was invigorating. It was a wonderful novelty to be standing alone.

Three days had passed since she'd come home. Not one moment was spent alone. Although she cherished all of their good intentions, it smothered her. Joy lifted her face to the wind, feeling it pass over her and through her unbound hair. With her eyes closed, she urged herself to feel, to really feel.

Emotions flowed over her in the same way the wind she did. The wall she'd built wouldn't come down. She tried, Lord knows she tried. She wanted to feel passion in each kiss and tenderness in each caress. She wanted to feel excitement about the baby. Only with Dillon did her reserve leave her.

She knew that Stamos sensed her withdrawal. He'd often just sit and look at her as if she was a puzzle he was trying to solve. Joy knew he felt it in her kiss and it frustrated her. She waited for his hurt to provoke her, but it didn't. Her heart had turned to ice and she didn't know how to thaw it.

She heard Stamos' footsteps walking toward her. Joy didn't turn, she didn't know what to say. He put his hands around her waist and pulled her back against her as he kissed the side of her neck.

It shamed her that she couldn't melt against him. If anything, she stiffened. Stamos stopped kissing her, but he didn't let go.

"Stamos?"

"Yes?"

"Promise me something," she whispered.

"Anything."

"Stamos, don't let go. Just don't let go." Joy pulled out of his embrace and walked away. She hoped to God he'd ride it out with her, but she was afraid that her heart would never thaw.

*****

Stamos sighed heavily and watched her go. He'd been trying to be the most understanding husband in the world, but it was getting him nowhere.

When she looked at him, the lights of love, happiness, and mischief were missing. He missed her. When Joy was with Dillon, she changed into the woman he knew and loved. She smiled and played and loved his son, but with him, nothing.

Stamos now comprehended that Joy knew and was asking him to hold on. It was difficult. He still got a morning and evening kiss, but it lacked any iota of passion. It'd only been three days, he knew that he needed to remain patient, but damn it all, it was hard.

Pulling his hat over his forehead, he stalked to the barn. Hard work would make him feel better. He hoped it would get rid of his restlessness.

"Hey, Boss," Benji greeted. "Look what I got."

Stamos walked toward Benji and looked at the two one-hundred-dollar bills he held. "Where'd you get the cash?"

Benji smiled. "I'm a secret agent."

Stamos frowned. "What do you mean?"

"I'm Benji Bond 008. I am helping to eliminate the enemy," he proudly told Stamos.

"And who is the enemy?" Stamos asked, his stomach churning.

"The shes."

Stamos had a bad feeling. "Who are the shes?"

Benji laughed and turned red. "You know the ones with a nice rack."

"Who are you working for?"

"I never see them. I just hear them. We meet at the willow tree each night."

Stamos sighed. "Benji, you wouldn't hurt Joy, would you?"

Benji shook his head. "Joy is my friend. We talk about her all the time and they give me money."

Stamos didn't know what to say. He was disgusted that anyone would use Benji to get to Joy. "Okay, buddy. Why don't you put the quarter horses out to pasture for me?"

Benji puffed out his chest. "You got it, Boss."

Stamos needed reinforcements and he knew just the people to call. Walking toward the house he realized that the sun had just risen and it was going to be a hell of a long day.

*****

Stamos paced in his office. He was trying to wrap his mind around everything Benji said. He was extremely grateful to have friends willing to drop everything to come and help. Joy would have to know. Maybe it would get a rise out of her. At this point, anything was better than the wooden smile she constantly gave him.

He did have hope though. She'd asked him not to let go and he wouldn't. He'd been bitter and disconnected after his first marriage failed. He'd been so ambitious then. He wanted to make a name for himself. He went into deep undercover work, spending six months in prison, then a year working for mobsters. Looking back, he wondered how his ex had stayed married to him as long as she had.

A black SUV pulled up into the driveway and Stamos shot out of the house to greet his cavalry.

"Good to see you." Stamos greeted, shaking Hoss Hill's hand then David Wonder's. "You guys are looking good. I can't thank you enough for coming."

Hoss smiled widely, his blond, blue-eyed look helped him to charm the ladies. "All you had to do was call."

David looked serious. He was the brooder of the three with dark hair cut military style and dark eyes. "Let's get on with the task at hand. I want to get these guys."

"I knew I could count on both of you," Stamos said, leading them inside.

Bea looked at the large men and her jaw dropped.

"Find Joy for me, Bea. I need her in the office."

"I sure will."

"Thanks." Stamos showed David and Hoss into his office.

"You wanted to see..." Joy trailed off as she looked at Hoss and David.

"Joy, I want you to meet some friends of mine." Stamos grabbed her hand and pulled her into the room. "This is Hoss and this is David. They are going to help us out."

Joy nodded her head absently to both men. Stamos wanted to laugh at Hoss' expression. Finally, a female that didn't drool over him.

"Joy, have a seat."

Joy looked a bit startled. "This sounds serious."

Stamos waited until everyone was seated. He sat on the arm of the chair next to Joy. "Someone has been paying Benji for information about you. He had two hundred-dollar bills. He said he is now Benji Bond and females are the enemy."

"Oh no." Joy's hand flew to her mouth. "Oh poor Benji. Who?" Her eyes widened with surprise that was quickly replaced with anger. "Excuse me gentlemen. I have some varmints that need killing."

Stamos grabbed Joy by the arm and sat her back down. "That's what we intend to do -- we'll hunt them down. Hoss and David worked with me at the FBI. They are top notch at what they do."

Joy studied both men, and then nodded. "So what's the plan?"

Her anger gave Stamos comfort. She was still in there, somewhere. He'd have to wait for her love to emerge. It was more hope than he had earlier.

"The plan is for you to stay out of it," Stamos said without thinking. The look on her face grew mutinous and he knew he was in for trouble.

"Now you wait one cotton picking minute Mr. Ex-lawman," Joy said as she jabbed her finger into his chest. "This is my fight."

Stamos grabbed her finger. "That hurts."

"Looks like I got here right on time," Callie announced, walking up to Stamos and grabbing his hand away from Joy's finger.

"What brings you here?" He stood and kissed her on the cheek.

"Move over Joy, I need to sit next to you and help you against these bulldozing men."

Joy smiled as she moved over and made room for Callie on the couch. "Really, why are you here?" Joy asked.

"A little birdie told me that you were outnumbered around here," she replied. Looking at Stamos she asked, "Don't you have any normal sized friends?"

Stamos laughed. "I guess she's not impressed with us."

Hoss just stared at her, unbelieving. "I don't know what you mean?"

"Too much testosterone in this room. What's going on and how can I help?" Callie asked.

Joy grabbed her hand as if it was a lifeline. She looked calmer.

David stared at Callie, he looked disapproving. "Is this going to be a hen party?" he grumbled.

Stamos had to bite his lips to keep from smiling. "Our main goal is to keep Joy safe."

"All of us safe," Joy amended.

Stamos smiled at her mutinous face. "Yes, all of us. They don't know we are on to them and I have a plan to keep Benji in the house most of the night."

"Okay, what's the plan?" Callie eagerly asked.

"Joy is going to need help babysitting Dillon. I'm sending Bea home with you tonight, Cal."

Joy shook her head. "That's your great plan?"

Hoss laughed, his blue eyes twinkling. "They are not impressed by you either my friend."

"It is a small part of the plan," Stamos said. "Since Wood and Jamie have Benji convinced that he is 008, why don't we give Benji a few gadgets? Mostly toy ones, but we can slip a microphone in something."

"Good, that's good," David said.

"What about me?" Callie asked.

Stamos laughed. "You my friend are going home to your husband. Does he even know you are here?"

"Who do you think sent me?"

Stamos raised one eyebrow, staring at her.

"Well he did after I insisted and threatened to make him sleep on the couch."

"I appreciate the support, Callie. I never had a friend before and it means a lot that you came. I guess the plan for tonight is set. I'll call you tomorrow and let you know how you can help," Joy told her, her words heartfelt.

"I'll go and take Bea with me, but I'll be back tomorrow. Don't you worry, Joy, I have been in this very position before. Men think that they need to keep the female safe. I'll be back."

Joy shared an amused glance with Stamos. "Let's go get Bea ready, and then I have to go get Benji."

"Gentlemen, I will see you tomorrow. I look forward to working with you," Callie said as she exited the room.

"She's kidding right?" Hoss asked.

Stamos shook his head. "I'm afraid not."

*****

With a lighter heart, Joy smiled, putting Dillon in Benji's arms. He was sitting in the middle of the couch with pillows on each side. He looked terrified. "It's just a baby," Joy said, sitting next to the pillow.

"I still don't know why you can't."

"Sit back and relax. See, Benji, he's smiling at you." Joy watched Benji begin to beam with pride. "I can't hold him, he keeps pulling my bandage off," Joy said, touching her bandaged cheek. She hadn't asked the doctor if she would have a scar, she didn't want to know. If she had to take in any more facts, she thought her brain would explode.

"I think he likes me," Benji exclaimed.

Joy smiled a real smile. It was a wonder, this big bear of a man holding Dillon so gently. "Of course he likes you, what's not to like?"

Benji's face turned serious. "I'm not like other folks. I used to be. I was smart as a whip. Now, I'm just not smart."

"That's not true. Benji, you are a kind loving man that is a great friend. You are great with the horses and I know that Stamos values you."

Benji smiled again. He didn't say anything, he just kept looking at Dillon in wonder. Dillon would babble and Benji acted as if he knew what Dillon was saying. Maybe he did, Joy mused.

Looking at the clock, she wondered how Hoss and David were doing. They were to watch the meeting site. They wanted to be sure that the information was accurate before they proceeded. It wouldn't do any good to haul Wood and Jaime into jail. They'd just deny everything.

"Let's go upstairs and get this little one ready for bed. I always read him a story or two." The wistful look in Benji's eyes almost made her tear up. "I'd appreciate it if you stayed until Stamos comes back." The smile she got in return humbled her.

*****

Stamos smiled as he peeked into Dillon's room. Benji must have carried Bea's rocking chair into the room. Dillon was in his crib awake, just watching the two adults in their chairs sleeping. Stamos backed away quietly. He needed to shower before he tended to Dillon. Hopefully Dillon would just fall asleep.

The hot water running down his head, shoulders, and back made him sigh. It had been a long day. All days had seemed extra-long. It would be worth it once he proved Joy's innocence.

Joy, just the thought of her made his chest tighten -- among other parts of his body. She looked angelic in the rocking chair, her hair loosely hanging down her shoulders. He wished that she would cling to him instead of pushing him away. Somehow, he knew she couldn't help it, but at times, it hurt.

He'd come to expect a look of love from her. He missed her smile and how her eyes glowed especially for him. There had to be a way to reach her.

The water had begun to grow cold as Stamos grabbed a towel in the steam-filled bathroom. It took him a few seconds to realize that he wasn't alone. Joy stood just inside the door staring at him. It seemed to be a look of desire, but Stamos was afraid to read too much into it.

Her big hazel eyes started at his toes and slowly raked up the length of him. He instantly hardened and the flare in her eyes made him realize that she noticed.

"Stamos?" she whispered, her voice shaky.

"What is it, love? I'm right here for you," Stamos told her in a steady voice. He was half afraid that she'd vanish through the steam.

Joy walked over and took the towel from his hands. She started at the middle of his chest, drying him off. Her tongue licked her lips as her hand holding the towel began to wander downward.

Stamos groaned. It took all of his control to stand there, allowing her to take the lead. If he had his choice she'd be bent over the sink right now, but it wasn't his choice. He closed his eyes as she dried and caressed his hip, he thought he was going out of his mind.

Dillon's cry shattered the moment. Joy dropped the towel. She gave Stamos a long look, up and down his body, and left.

Stamos shuddered in need. His breathing had become labored. Running his hand over his face, he turned the cold water on. He needed to cool off.

*****

Joy shook Benji's shoulder and told him to go back to the bunkhouse. She thanked him and he smiled at her praise. Picking up Dillon, she gently cooed to him. Her heart beat out of her chest. She kept seeing Stamos dripping wet, an image that wouldn't shake loose. Smiling, Joy wasn't sure she wanted to shake it loose.

She changed Dillon's diaper and sat down in the rocking chair with Dillon in one arm and his bottle in her other hand.

"Ma Ma, Ma Ma," he chanted, trying to reach for her hair.

"You are a little rascal, just like your daddy." Joy fed Dillon. Feelings she didn't even know she had exploded in her heart. Her whole body tingled with happiness. Tears ran down her face, she'd never known such happiness. This time she actually had blessings to count.

Her shoulders shook as she cried, silently sobbing as she continued to feed Dillon. She, of all people knew that you might not get a tomorrow, and knowing that she had wasted precious moments made her cry all the harder.

She heard Stamos enter the room, but she couldn't look at him. She'd been cold and shut off from him and she felt so guilty for her feelings.

"Joy? Are you hurt?" Stamos asked.

The concern in his voice was too much for her. She handed Dillon to him and took off down the stairs and out the front door. She ran until she was at the edge of the yard. She couldn't breathe. She had treated Stamos, the one person who loved her, so horribly.

Her eyes burned and she began to hiccup. Closing her eyes, she raised her face to the night sky and tried to slow her breathing. What if it was too late? What if Stamos couldn't forgive her cold heartlessness? Did he still love her?

How she wished she knew more about relationships. Obviously she wasn't good at them. She was out of her element. Freedom came with a lot of new feelings, good feelings and scary feelings. Joy wasn't sure if she could cope.

Opening her eyes, she hugged herself, trying to keep herself in one piece. The Texas sky looked big and comforting. The moon appeared so big, Joy wanted to reach out and touch it. A star shot across the black sky.

"You're supposed to make a wish," Stamos told her, walking behind her and pulling her back against him.

Joy leaned back. She was not alone. It was something she had known, but had never taken to heart. Now she had Stamos. She wasn't in this big universe alone anymore.

Turning in his arms, she wrapped her arms around his waist and just laid her head over his heart. She could feel his big hands rubbing up and down her back, soothing her. Never had she had such comfort. "Forgive me?" she asked, pulling away to look at his face.

"Oh, baby, you know when I look in your eyes I see the future. I see our happiness. Joy, I love you. Of course I forgive you. All of this has taken a toll on you. I know that. I've been waiting for my Joy to come back, and here you are."

Joy didn't have time to reply before Stamos swooped down and kissed her. It was a searing kiss of possession and Joy loved it. This time she put her tongue in his mouth first and she tingled as he groaned.

His response empowered her. Stepping closer she pushed her hips against his and bumped against his hard desire. A flicker of excitement burst within her body. There seemed a strange urgency, an immense hunger in his kiss. He stopped kissing her lips and started kissing her neck, making her shiver in delight. Her legs gave way when he blew into her ear.

Stamos swung her up into his brawny arms. Joy felt so loved, so safe. She would always treasure this moment. Reaching up, she stroked his face. His face was rough with whiskers. The desire that she could see in his eyes made her breasts feel heavy. His sexy grin made her nipples tighten.

"Are you sure?" Stamos asked his voice husky with desire.

Joy nodded her head. "I need you, Stamos. I love you."

"Oh God," Stamos moaned. "I didn't know if I'd hear those words from you again."

"Me neither," Joy admitted. "I want to go to bed."

"Sleepy are ya?" Stamos teased.

"Not so much, I want to make love with my husband," she whispered, blowing into his ear. His arms tightened around her as he hurried toward the house.

Stamos put her on her feet just inside the front door. He looked at her long and hard. "Are you sure?"

Joy stepped forward and reached up, entwining her fingers in his hair, bringing his face down to her level. Licking her lips, she looked at him. She moved in and nibbled at his bottom lip.

"Umm. I'm taking that as a yes," Stamos said, as his breathing became heavy. Picking her up, he carried her up to their bedroom.

"Aren't you going to turn on the light?" she asked, as he laid her on the bed.

"No time, love. I need you now."

Joy smiled. "Then why are we still dressed?"

Stamos laughed. "Hell if I know." He removed her clothes.

He acted as though he was unwrapping a precious present and Joy felt cherished. Reaching up she unbuttoned his shirt and started on his belt buckle. She found Stamos' hands already there.

"God you are beautiful," he groaned.

"It's dark."

"I can see you in the moonlight. A sight to behold."

"Really?" she asked, not quite believing him.

Stamos settle himself between her legs. "Believe me." He thrust into her.

"Deeper, oh, Stamos, please."

Stamos kissed her neck then took one rosy nipple into his mouth. Joy arched her back wanting more. She began to move her hips faster trying to take him deeper. "You feel so good," she cried.

The world exploded around her. Joy was spinning out of control. She heard cries of pleasure. Looking into Stamos' eyes, she could see his soul. He loved her.

*****

Watching her sleep humbled Stamos. Her reaction, her passion, far exceeded anything he could have hoped. It also scared him. How long would it last? Only until she got skittish again? Would she pull away again and hide her emotions? She had the ability to push her feelings so deep and far inside that there had been times he didn't think he'd have his wife back. This last time, since she went back to prison, had been hell. He understood, but he didn't know if his heart could take her rejection again.

He wondered if she was pleased that she carried his child. Joy never brought up the subject. She treated Dillon so lovingly. Something was a bit off. Oh hell, who was he fooling? Everything has seemed off since he opened that door and found her standing there.

Maybe she didn't want his child. Maybe she didn't want to tie herself to him any tighter. Stamos sighed, he didn't know what to think.

All he was doing was torturing himself with doubts. Hadn't they just made love?

He felt so protective of her. She could hold her own, but she wasn't alone anymore. She was his to protect.

The blanket had slipped down so that it just covered Joy's delicious breasts. So many scars. So many bruises. Damn her father. How could a father put a hit on his own daughter? He knew he was missing the key to the whole sordid mess. Money is a good motive, but in this case, there had to be more to it. He could feel it in his gut.

Joy stirred and cried out in her sleep. She quieted when Stamos drew her against him, tucking her head under his chin. He wrapped his arms around her. Sighing, Joy settled down. Stamos wished he could wake her and make love to her again, but she needed her sleep. She was carrying his child. Eventually slumber claimed him.

*****

Joy held Dillon. She had to make sure he didn't pull at her bandaged cheek. So far, she'd been able to distract him. Hearing a truck drive up, Joy eagerly went out the door hoping it was Bea and Callie. She'd been feeling uncertain since waking up alone. Stamos had been AWOL all morning. His absence made her nervous.

Smiling, she walked out to the front porch. Bea got out of the truck looking none too happy.

"You'd better go reassure your friend," she said. She took Dillon and went into the house.

Confused, Joy walked toward the truck and was surprised to see Garrett driving. "Hi guys."

"Tell her," Garrett told Callie.

Callie's blue eyes looked defiant as she shifted her gaze from Joy to her husband. Sighing she turned toward Joy. "I can't stay. I know you need me, but my husband here is being a jack--"

"Now just a darn second," Garrett objected. "Listen Joy, Wonder Woman can't play today."

"Oh, for God's sake," Callie exclaimed, with fire in her eyes.

"Callie left those munchkins with me all day yesterday. I have a lot of work to do. I don't mind a day here or there, but I really have things that need to be done today."

"Listen, don't fight on my account. Callie, I understand, I'm married to a rancher too. Who is watching Rose and Aiden now?"

"Old Henry," Garrett said, trying not to laugh.

"Y'all better get home. Your twins go running in different directions," Joy said good naturedly, trying to cut the tension.

"See, I told you they do that," Garrett insisted.

"Joy, you call me if you need me. If there is a will, there is a way."

"Bye, Joy." Garrett turned the truck around and sped down the drive.

Joy watched them drive away. They were a good couple, even when they disagreed. The image of Old Henry trying to corral those twins had Joy laughing by the time she went back to the house.

Chapter Eleven

The old wooden clock in the kitchen tic-tocked incessantly all morning. It had never bothered Joy before, but today she was aware of each movement of the second hand. Bea, bless her heart, was busy chatting away about pie making. Joy just smiled and nodded.

Dillon napped and Joy wanted to jump out of her skin. Still she waited for Stamos to come home. Her stomach was a mess, all tied in knots. Why had he left without saying goodbye? What happened to a kiss in the morning?

Wringing her hands, she wanted to weep. Damn hormones, they made her feel uneasy. They made her feel, and that alone was making her crazy. Where was Stamos? Did he regret last night?

"Joy, the clock isn't going to move any faster with you watching it," Bea told her.

Joy gave her a brief smile. "You're right. I just wonder where Stamos went."

"Why not call him? He carries one of those high-tech phones."

Joy just shook her head. She'd thought of that already, but decided that if he wanted to talk to her he would have called. It became obvious to her that he didn't want to talk to her, or kiss her.

Taking a deep breath, Joy tried to put him out of her mind. She looked around the old worn kitchen and smiled. It was her favorite room in the house. Stamos hadn't gotten around to remodeling it yet and she hoped he wouldn't. The wood counters had names carved into them by a not so sharp jack-knife. Joy often wondered if someone had caught hell for doing it. All the appliances were on their last legs, but for now, they worked. Bea seemed happy enough with the kitchen. She often remarked how big it was.

Where was Stamos? The doubts became too much for her. Joy went into their bedroom and sat on the bed, pulling his pillow to her. She smelled the pillow and closed her eyes. It smelled of him -- sexy, clean, and leather.

Pregnancy didn't agree with her. The baby was turning her into a weak ninny and she couldn't stand it. Looking in the mirror, Joy examined her face. She looked the same on the outside. There was no sign of the uncertain pansy that she had become on the inside. In fact, she felt like a crazy shrew on top of it all.

Hearing a truck door slam, Joy hurried downstairs. She hoped to have Stamos to herself for a while, but the closing of other truck doors burst her bubble. When she walked into the kitchen, she noticed Hoss and David. Giving them a quick nod, she set her eyes on Stamos.

He looked at her and then looked away. Where were the tender loving looks from last night? What had she done wrong? He didn't even greet her and there was no good morning kiss.

"Let's go into my office," he said briskly.

Joy wasn't sure if the invitation included her. She followed anyway and sat down on the couch. This time Stamos didn't sit next to her. He leaned against the front of his desk looking angry.

"Those bastards were here again last night," Stamos said angrily.

"My--"

"I have a plan," Stamos stated, cutting Joy off.

Joy sat back and looked away. Stamos was acting as though she wasn't even in the room. She wished she could turn numb, but it wasn't working. The pain became intense.

"Let's have it," David Wonder said.

Hoss smiled, looking just as eager. They seemed to be enjoying their work. Somehow, it made Joy resentful. It wasn't reasonable, but it seemed as though they were getting off on her problems.

The room was quiet and Joy blushed. They were all looking at her. "What? Did I miss something?"

"Joy, this is all about you. Pay attention," Stamos said.

She could see the disgust in his eyes. Cringing, she apologized.

"I want you to tell Benji how cool all his new spy stuff is."

"What new spy stuff?"

"Joy, if you aren't going to help then leave."

Her eyes began to burn with unshed tears. How could he act this way? What had she done wrong? This Stamos she didn't know. She wanted her husband back. "I'll help in any way I can."

"I still think we should just keep your wife out of it," Hoss commented, glancing at Joy with a frown.

"It'll work out better my way. Benji likes Joy."

Now she knew she had to be imagining things. Stamos had made it sound surprising that Benji would like her. What was going on?

"Fine, you're the boss. Just let us know where and when," David said.

Hoss nodded in agreement.

Funny, she had thought David the broody type. Hoss acted broody today. The room was closing in on her. Too many broad shoulders, she surmised.

Once again, she'd let her mind wander. She looked up to see Hoss and Davis shaking hands with Stamos. Stamos turned and looked at her. The disappointment in his eyes became too much and tears trailed down her face. Her bandaged cheek stung as her salty tears reached it.

"Joy?"

"I have to change this bandage. My face hurts." She pushed against him in her hurry to get out of the office.

She heard him call her name again, but she couldn't go back. She needed to figure out what she'd done to make Stamos treat her so cruelly.

*****

Leaning against the door jam, Stamos admitted that he acted like a first class heel. Joy's hands were shaking so hard that she was having trouble with her bandage. He cursed softly and pushed away from the door. He took the bandage out of Joy's hands.

The look on her face didn't surprise him. It was a mixture of surprise and distrust. "Let me do that."

Joy just looked at him without saying a word.

Seeing her sadness, Stamos felt awful. Why couldn't he get anything right? Last night had been so special, too special, and it scared him. She'd left him before and all day he worried that she'd light out again.

Gently cleaning her wound, Stamos could smell her clean essence. Her scent reminded him of wildflowers. He gazed at her ripe lips, wanting to capture them with his own. Looking into her eyes cured him of that desire.

Stamos wished he knew the words to make her feel better. His first wife left and Joy had already left him once. Try as he might, he couldn't shake it. He'd work it out, he always did. He just hoped that he didn't kill his marriage in the process.

"There. All bandaged," he announced, taking a step back.

"Okay," Joy said woodenly.

"Joy, I'm sorry. I don't--"

Joy put her hand up to ward off any more of his words. "I can't talk to you about this right now. I know what you're going to say and right now I'm not strong enough to hear it."

Stamos wasn't sure what she meant, but he nodded his head and walked out of the room. He didn't know what to say to her. He had a lot of work to do. He hoped to work some of the uneasiness out of him.

*****

Joy tried to look excited when Benji showed her all of his spy stuff. He had a mirror that could see around corners, which they both used to spy on Bea while she made a pie. Bea knew what was going on, but she played innocent.

He next showed her his night vision goggles. They both had to go in and out of the windowless bathroom to use them. Benji was pleased as punch.

"What's this?" Joy asked, looking at a toy car.

"This is the best. It takes pictures, you know like a movie, and it goes when I punch this button."

Benji took the remote and next thing Joy knew, the remote controlled car was chasing her. She was glad that she wasn't wearing a dress. She wasn't sure where the camera was, but she hoped it wouldn't be invasive.

"It is the best," Joy enthused. "But we have to be careful with this one."

Benji's smile disappeared. "Why?"

"This could trip a person, or scare a horse even. I'm sure a spy like you knows that already."

Benji smiled proudly. "Yep."

"What's this?" Joy asked, picking up a shiny pen.

"That is a magic pen that writes upside down. Stamos told me to keep it in my pocket all the time," Benji explained seriously.

"You are lucky to have a pen like that," Joy told him. She knew that it had a microphone and a GPS in it.

"These night goggles are going to come in handy tonight."

"Why is that, Benji?"

"Spies never tell."

"I guess you're right. I just want you to be safe. I wouldn't want one of my favorite friends hurt."

Benji puffed out his chest. "I can take care of myself. Stamos has taught me a lot. In prison they called me dumb, but you know what, Joy? I'm not. I can do all kinds of things and I help make this ranch run."

"Oh, Benji, of course you make this place run. We couldn't do it without you."

Stamos watched them. He shared a smile with her, until she recalled that she was mad at him. Her smile quickly turned into a frown. Blast him for making her forget.

His smile turned into a frown too and Joy wondered about it. What a moody man he turned out to be.

"A lot of cool stuff," Stamos said. He stood next to Joy and took her hand in his.

Joy was tempted to pull away, but she didn't want to upset Benji. His nearness made her tingle and her heart beat rapidly. Joy tried to conjure up her anger. To her dismay, it was draining out of her.

"Oh my. Oh my," Bea exclaimed, from the kitchen.

Stamos pulled Joy along to see what the problem was. They both stood inside the kitchen doorway and laughed.

Nanny and Nino had somehow gotten into the kitchen and were helping themselves to apples and pie. "How'd they get in here?" Joy asked in amazement.

"I didn't invite them. I went upstairs to check on the little mister and when I came back down here they were eating my afternoon's work."

Joy looked at Stamos whose lips were twitching. She tried to look sympathetic to Bea's outrage, but in the end, she couldn't. Joy laughed so she had to hold her stomach. Suddenly she stopped laughing. Something inside her moved. It felt as though there was a butterfly inside her.

She looked at Stamos, then at Bea. "I'm pregnant," she said in awe.

Stamos gathered her close to him and kissed her. He picked her up and started walking.

"Where are we going?"

"Upstairs to talk. Benji, could you get Nanny and Nino out of the kitchen?"

"Sure thing, Stamos. You can count on me."

*****

"Put me down and not on the bed," Joy demanded.

"Aw, honey, I thought--"

"That's your problem. You are either thinking wrong or you are thoughtless."

Stamos put her down turning her to face him. Her hazel eyes were blazing. "Okay, I'll bite, what's wrong? Is it your hormones?"

Joy marched over to the door and held it open. "Bye."

"What's wrong, Joy? I guess I don't understand why you are so damn mad?"

Joy's face crumbled. "Don't you dare make me cry. I'm running out of bandages for my face."

"You don't want the baby?" Stamos asked, feeling put out.

Joy touched her abdomen and her look of awe came back, but she didn't look at him.

"If it's not the baby then what is your problem?"

Joy marched up to Stamos. "My problem is you -- you big jerk."

Stamos tried to put his arms around her.

"Don't touch me. It doesn't mean anything when you touch me."

Stamos gave her a hard look. Granted he'd been busy all day, but he didn't deserve this. "Let's start over. Tell me what is wrong. Tell me what I did to make you so angry." Stamos sat on the side of the bed.

Joy looked at him. She stared, trying to read him. She opened her mouth starting to speak, and quickly closed it again. She sighed deeply and immense hurt showed in her eyes.

"Am I so insensitive that I hurt you and don't know about it?"

Joy looked away then she looked into his eyes. Her face softened briefly, and then it was full of anger again.

"God knows I have never been able to read a woman's mind. I thought everything was going great between us. My God, last night was wonderful," he said.

"Was it?" Joy asked, folding her arms before her.

"All right, Joy, out with it. What major crime did I commit?"

"You make me feel shrewish. You want to know what you did? It's the way you've acted toward me today. I've never been closer to anyone like last night. This morning I wake up and you've turned cold and hard. No good morning kiss. Hell, not even a smile. So don't go talking to me about hormones or supposed hurts. I am hurt."

Stamos got up off the bed. "Joy..." He walked toward her. "I'm sorry. I'm a buffoon." He stood in front of her, but not too close. He wanted to give her room. "I've, well, oh hell. Part of me is ecstatic about last night and part of me is scared to death."

Joy shook her head, looking into his eyes. "I don't understand."

Stamos ran his fingers through his hair, gazing at her. "Why should you understand? I haven't even explained anything to you. I've been waiting and hoping for the closeness and passion we found last night. This morning I felt afraid that I loved you too much and you'd end up leaving me."

Joy's eyes misted as she looked at him. Her smile lit up her whole face. "No matter what you always demanded a morning kiss..."

"I'm sorry, babe." Stamos pulled her into his arms and kissed her. He intended to brand her. He wanted Joy to feel his love in that one kiss. From her response, he could tell he succeeded.

She snaked her arms around his neck and held on. Her tongue in his mouth made him crazy. Her moans excited him and when she pushed her hips against his, he thought he'd jump out of his skin.

Little by little, he let her go. Looking into her eyes, he could see stars. "I'm a jackass. Forgive me?"

Joy blushed and nodded. "Just don't forget my goodnight kiss."

"Never again. I promise I won't forget again. I think we need to talk though." He could tell by her frown that she was expecting the worst. "You sometimes seem so distant to me. There are whole days that I think that I have lost you. I understand prison mentality, really I do. You always give your love to Dillon and that's great. It's just that I feel hurt that I'm not included in your unconditional love," Stamos confessed, looking into her big eyes.

"Unconditional love? I'm afraid I don't know what that is."

Stamos smiled and took her hand. Entwining his fingers with hers, he bought her small hand to his mouth and he kissed it. "It's the love you give to Dillon. It's the love that you give with no strings attached. It's when your heart is full of the other person no matter what mistakes they make. It includes forgiveness and giving the benefit of the doubt. It's knowing that no matter what, the one you love is always on your side. They always have your back."

Joy's eyes never left his face. It was almost as though he could see the very moment when she understood what he was saying.

"You have unconditional love for me?" she inquired.

"Without a doubt," he replied seriously.

"My heart is going to burst, Stamos. I never want to be without you. I do love you."

Stamos pulled her into his arms and hugged her. He loved the feel of her in his arms. She didn't know it, but she had allayed all of his fears. She had no wiles, no agenda. Joy just was.

"I can feel the baby moving," she whispered.

"You do want the baby don't you?"

Joy pulled away and smiled. The whole room lit up under that one smile. "Of course I do. It didn't seem real to me before. Now," she stoked her abdomen, "now it's fluttering around inside me and I feel so blessed. So yes, Stamos, I'm happy about the baby. I'm proud to be carrying your baby."

A wail from Dillon interrupted the moment they shared. "Let's go and see to our son," Stamos suggested.

Joy smiled and nodded.

*****

Joy looked out into the eerie night feeling anxious. Her father and brother were dangerous and she didn't want Stamos going after them. If they were to live in peace, they had no choice. Still, it made her nervous.

Dillon was tucked in for the night and Bea had gone to her room. Stamos, Hoss, and David all left together. Stamos had given her one hell of a kiss before he left. Touching her lips with her fingers, she shivered.

Then there was Benji. What if he got hurt? She'd never forgive herself. Joy couldn't seem to help being fretful. She observed a shadow moving across the yard. Her gut told her that she was in danger.

Moving slowly, she went to Stamos' desk and opened the top drawer. Joy sighed in relief when she spotted the handgun. Picking it up, she tucked it into the waistband of her pants, in the back. Her heart was in her throat and she could barely swallow. Who could it be? Probably her no good, mangy family.

Why wouldn't they just let her be? Her whole body tensed as she waited in the shadows, watching. Her nerves were getting to her and she began to shake.

The front door handle rattled and turned. Joy took the gun into her hand and pointed at the door. She held it with both hands, trying not to shake so much.

The door swung open and Joy held her breath. She was ready. She had Dillon to protect. She could do this. The door opened all the way, yet the person hadn't entered the house.

With her heart thumping out of her chest, Joy took a step toward the door and almost shot at the intruder when he entered the house. It had been a close thing. She'd almost shot Benji.

With her adrenaline waning, Joy leaned back against the sofa cushion and closed her eyes. She'd almost shot at Benji. The horror of it made her shake. Crossing her arms in front, she hugged herself, trying to keep from coming apart.

Benji happily drank the hot cocoa that Bea had made him. The seriousness of her actions didn't envelope him. Joy was grateful for his naivety.

Stamos had entered the house not long after Benji and he immediately took the gun from her. She hadn't even realized that she still held it. At least he wasn't angry. He seemed almost sympathetic.

Now Hoss, David, and George were all huddled together, talking. Talking about her. Joy smiled at George. His hug helped her to regain her sanity, once again.

Too bad George hadn't come under better circumstances. Bea was all doe eyed with him around. He looked right back at her. Joy made a mental note to get them together after all the craziness stopped. If all the craziness stopped. The looks on the men's faces didn't look too promising. Her need to run away was growing greater and greater, but she couldn't leave Stamos. He'd told her his fears and she planned to be a safe keeper of his secrets.

"I should have used my see around the corner mirror. Then I'd have know'd that you were in here with the gun," Benji said.

"Benji, it's not your fault. I overreacted. I'm just glad that you didn't get hurt," Joy told him.

"You don't understand. Nothing can hurt agent 008."

Joy's eyes flew to Stamos' face in alarm. He must have heard what Benji said. He immediately left the huddle and walked over to them. Putting an arm around Benji, Stamos smiled at him.

"Even secret agents can get hurt, Benji. It's best to be careful. You'd better go get some shut-eye, buddy. Tomorrow will be here before we know it."

"Sure thing, Stamos," Benji agreed as he left the house.

The couch dipped under Stamos' weight. "How's my beautiful wife?" he inquired.

Joy didn't trust herself to speak. She turned and buried her face in his shoulder instead and knew instant comfort when Stamos wrapped his arms around her. She needed a plan to keep them all safe. She loved them all.

"They didn't show tonight. I don't know what that means," Stamos admitted.

Joy didn't reply. She was too busy trying to find her inner strength. She'd find it in the circle of Stamos' arms.

"Hey we found something," George announced.

Stamos jumped off the couch, pulling Joy along with them.

"They were there earlier. Sounds like they had a fight and left before Benji got there," Hoss explained.

Joy could see the excitement in the men's eyes. "Well?"

"I placed a bug in the tree that they usually meet at," David explained, with a smile. "Listen to this."

David pushed a button on his computer and everyone was quiet.

"I'm getting tired of this," Jamie's voice was loud and clear.

"Leave, I don't need you. You've become a whiner just like your sister." Joy's eyes widened when she heard her father's voice.

"I'm not so sure that's true. She hasn't opened her mouth and I don't think she will," Jamie said.

"Look, you got that bitch Bailey involved. If she hadn't called that Stacey slut, we'd have been fine. We can't have the law looking into Joy's case. You know it," her father yelled.

"How was I supposed to know that Stacey would want custody? I'm about done. I covered for you, but Joy has paid a very high price for your actions," Jaime said his voice full of disgust.

"You just don't get it. If she opens her mouth, we both go down. You are as much a part of this as I am. We'll use Benji, find out when she'll be alone, and we'll take her."

Joy's hand flew to her mouth in dismay. It was one thing to know, but hearing it was almost unbearable. She couldn't fathom what she had done to her father to have him hate her so. She'd thought about it plenty over the years.

"I thought I took the fall for Jaime. It sounds like..." Joy began to weep.

Stamos pulled her close. "Sounds like your son of a bitch father did the killing."

Joy nodded against his shoulder. The salty tears on her cut cheek went unnoticed as her heart broke. Even after all her father had done, the little girl inside her still held out hope. She'd thought herself past such hurts. The pain in her heart was proof that it wasn't true.

"Joy? Joy, are you all right?" Stamos asked.

"I shouldn't be surprised. I shouldn't even be hurt, but it does hurts. It hurts big time," she cried.

"Some hurts just never go away, Joy. Let's go upstairs and get some rest," Stamos suggested.

Joy nodded and woodenly followed Stamos, glad that he was holding her hand.

Once upstairs, Joy's tears faded. Stamos had taken off his shirt and she couldn't help but stare. Every muscle was so well defined. She loved his abs. The thought of touching him sent shivers through her body.

What was wrong with her? One minute her world seemed to be crumbling around her and now, all she could think of was how good Stamos could make her feel. Stepping closer, Joy reached out with a shaking hand and touched his chest. The hair on it looked so sexy and it was soft.

She wanted to be naked against his skin. Suddenly it became too much. A sense of urgency shot through her. Stamos smiled at her and it was all the encouragement she needed to ravage her man.

Reaching up, Joy pulled his head down to her lips, kissing him deeply, her tongue invading his mouth.

Stamos tensed for a moment, and then relaxed. He wrapped his loving arms around her and pulled her close.

It wasn't close enough for Joy. She broke their kiss to tear off her top and rip off her bra. The fire was intense, burning so hot. She made quick work of her jeans and panties too. Seeing that Stamos was taking off his clothes pleased her.

Joy pushed him down on the bed and got on top of him, kissing his lush, sensual lips. She kissed her way down his body, loving his moans of pleasure. He surprised her and sat her on top of him.

Yes, this is what she wanted. The faster the better. Joy had never known such passion, such desire. It blocked out all else. The world was just her and Stamos, making sweet love. Faster and faster, until she cried out in pleasure.

Joy looked into his dark eyes, not knowing what to expect. Stamos' eyes were passion filled and his smile made him look to be a very satisfied man.

"That was--"

Joy put her finger over his lips. "Don't talk. Let's just feel." She snuggled against him and cherished the feeling of being in his arms.

It was such a strange feeling. It felt identical to coming home and it humbled Joy as Stamos stroked her back. This cowboy had given her more than any other person. He'd given her a home and his heart. Then there was Dillon and the baby growing inside her.

"I love you," she whispered.

*****

Rinsing out her mouth, Joy recognized that being pregnant wasn't all it seemed cracked up to be. She looked in the mirror for that special glow she'd heard about. All she could see was a pale, tired woman glaring back at her. It became hard to count her many blessings when she was constantly throwing up.

A car door slammed, then another. Joy groaned. She wanted to go back to bed and hide under the covers. Her heart warmed as she remembered the night before. She wasn't alone. She had Stamos and Dillon.

Women, it was women's voices she heard greeting Bea like an old friend. Curious, Joy plastered a smile on her face and stuck her tongue out at herself in the mirror. Somehow, it made her feel better.

Joy's smile became real when she walked into the kitchen. Two older women sat at the kitchen table, drinking tea. One had long black hair, which looked a bit odd with her aged face. The other looked grandmotherly.

Bea walked over, took Joy by the arm, and led her to the table. "Joy these are, the leading ladies of Lasso Springs, Harriett and Mable."

Joy smiled at them. "Nice to meet you."

"Of course it is, dear," Harriett said, flinging her hair around until it was slightly off center.

Joy bit back a laugh. Harriett's wig was outlandish.

"We've been wanting to come and meet you," Mable explained. "My son is the town's best lawyer--"

"Mable, she doesn't need a lawyer. We've come to greet you dear. We welcome you to our town. If you ever get to town, stop by my shop, Harriett's Yarn and Tea Shop. It's the town's hotspot."

"Thank you, ladies. You are both very kind," Joy said graciously.

"We also have gossip. That brother of yours is getting very friendly with that Bailey woman," Harriett blurted out.

"They've been courtin' and sparkin'. His truck is at her house overnight," Mable exclaimed.

Bea and Joy exchanged troubled looks. This couldn't be good. Joy had trouble concentrating on the two women after that. She was so lost in thought it surprised her when the two women stood and offered her hugs.

"You come on by and have some tea. I can teach you how to knit a few things for Dillon and the new baby," Harriet offered. Her hair looked straightened now.

"Thank you. Thank you both for taking the time to visit," Joy said.

Bea and Joy waved as the women got into their car and drove off.

"I don't like the sound of Jaime and Bailey being together," Bea said solemnly.

"Me neither."

*****

Stamos watched the wind blow through Joy's loose hair. She wasn't wearing her hat and it made her look sexy as hell. Her cheeks were apple red from the brisk autumn day. She'd been so pale lately. Stamos knew she was having bouts of morning sickness.

He'd thought she'd promised to stay in the house today. He loved her independent spirit, but not when there was danger. It was pure magic to see Joy with the horses. They followed her every command. A car had hit the particular horse she was with now, Ollie, and the owner hoped save it.

Ollie was fine physically, but his soul suffered. He'd become skittish and didn't want to be handled. Joy talked to him easily and Ollie allowed her to pat him. Stamos smiled. His wife was quite a woman.

His smile turned to a look of alarm as Joy swung up onto Ollie's bare back. It took all of his control to stay put. Running toward her would frighten the horse. Stamos' heart pounded out of his chest as he watched her. His gut clenched when Ollie bucked.

Joy leaned down and talked to him, calming him. What if she had been thrown? She could have lost the baby or hurt herself. Didn't she know how much she meant to him? How empty his life would be without her? He'd told her that he loved her, but did she believe it?

Joy sent him a radiant smile. He didn't have the heart to yell at her, not when she finally looked happy.

Stamos watched as she lowered herself from Ollie's back and walked toward him. Her smile didn't falter, but the shadows in her eyes told him that something was wrong.

"Nice riding," Stamos said, lifting Joy down off the fence.

"Thanks. I just needed to be outside for a bit," Joy said, sounding wary.

Stamos pulled her even closer and held her. "I understand. I do want to know what's bothering you."

Joy lifted her face to him and studied him. "How do you know that something is bothering me?"

Stamos leaned down and kissed her long and hard. "Because I know you. Somehow you've become part of me."

"I don't know what I did to deserve you," Joy murmured as she reached up and pulled his head down for another kiss.

"Jaime is shacking up with Bailey," Joy whispered.

"Like hell. Who told you that?"

"Harriett and Mable came a calling."

"Oh hell." He hugged her. "It's probably true, those two don't miss a thing."

Joy pulled away and looked into his eyes. "What do you think it means?"

"Nothing good, my love, nothing good."

"I didn't notice before, but I'm heavily guarded." Joy nodded toward Arlo, Kid, Hoss, and David.

"Can't have anything happen to my lovely wife."

"Am I?" She bit her lip.

"My wife?"

Joy shook her head. "Am I lovely? Somehow I think you lie."

Stamos felt surprised. "Haven't I told you before? You are the most lovely, beautiful, sexy woman I know. I've never been attracted to any woman the way I am attracted to you."

Joy blushed bright red. "I guess I've tried for most of my life to look unattractive that I've come to believed it."

"Trust me," Stamos said. "Let's get you and the little one out of the cold."

The smile she bestowed on him warmed his heart. They would be all right. Things would work out if he could only keep her safe.

*****

Joy had just finished getting Dillon to bed. Her heart almost burst when he chanted, Ma Ma, all through bath time. He was now all snuggly warm in his crib.

Bea had gone to bed early, leaving Joy on her own. The men were all out waiting and watching to see if Benji made contact with her family.

Some family, she lamented. They had duped her. For years, she wondered why. Then she wondered how she could be so stupid. It wasn't until lately that she comprehended she had been a young trusting girl who would do anything to help her family.

The feeling of betrayal cut deep. It was agony to know that they wanted her dead. She had loved them. Some hurts just never went away.

Joy's whole body tensed as she paced in the study. A wave of extreme exhaustion crashed over her. She had to know what the outcome of tonight's surveillance was. Putting Benji in potential harm ate at her. Her heart skipped a beat when she spotted the trucks coming up the drive. She didn't even grab a coat, she bolted out into the cold night.

Stamos was first to greet her with a nice hug. He urged her inside, insisting that everyone was safe. He led her to the couch and sat down next to her.

"Well? What happened?"

"Benji did real good."

"I sure did," Benji said, joining them.

"You're okay?" Joy asked.

Benji beamed at her concern. "Yes and best of all I was very clever."

Joy looked at Stamos who nodded.

"Benji was indeed clever. He told Wood and Jaime about Harriett and Mable's visit and all hell broke loose."

"Yeah. They fighted and yelled. It was good fun," Benji enthused.

"That's a good thing?" Joy asked, confused.

"Of course," Benji said, nodding his head at her.

"I don't get it."

"Having Wood and Jaime at each other's throat should help," Stamos explained.

"My father didn't know Jaime is shacking up with Bailey? Fireworks should be happening. Jaime never did anything my father disapproved of."

"That's what we're hoping for darlin'."

Chapter Twelve

"What time is your doctor's appointment?" Stamos finished his breakfast. Once again, he had more of Dillon's food on him than Dillon actually ate.

Joy laughed. "Not till one. Don't worry, I won't let you miss it. Why do you persist in feeding Dillon when you get so covered in baby food?"

Stamos looked down at his colorfully blotched shirt. "I enjoy being a hands on dad. Worked a bit better before he was on this baby food. I noticed it stains."

"Put an apron on. Dillon doesn't spit out his food at me." Her eyes met his shining ones and her heart melted.

Stamos stood and took Joy's hand. He gave it a slight tug. "Come give me a great big hug, Mrs. Walker. I need you next to me."

Joy laughed and shook her head. His sexy grin almost had her. "I'll give you all the hugs you need as soon as you change your shirt."

"You are a hard woman, Joy. What Dillon must think?" he admonished, his eyes twinkling.

"He thinks I'm wonderful." Joy grabbed a clean cloth from the table and began to wipe Dillon's mouth. He excitedly waved his hands in the air babbling.

"No, if you listen carefully you'll find that he's saying, Mommy, be good to Daddy."

Joy's heart expanded at their light banter. The last few days had been tense. Everyone had a different plan to get her father and brother in jail. Even George had been a constant presence. Joy loved the way he and Bea looked at each other. There were plenty of blushes between the two, and Joy wondered if Bea had been stepping out with George.

"Go. I'll hug you in a bit."

"Promise?" he asked quietly.

"Always," she whispered back.

Stamos took a step toward her and grabbed her around the waist. Joy was outraged as his brawny arms captured her into a big hug. He rubbed his chest against hers, causing her insides to spark. Stamos' lips on hers silenced any protest.

Joy couldn't win. Right now, she didn't want to. Wrapping her arms around his neck, she pulled his in for a deeper kiss. His tongue in her mouth made her moan in pleasure. Whispers of excitement flickered through her body. Her breasts became heavy and very sensitive. Flames were licking at her lower abdomen.

Stamos made love to her mouth. His arousal pressed hard against her. Joy wanted him with a heightened sense of desire. She wondered if it was because of her pregnancy.

The sounds of Dillon yelling "Da Da," broke them apart. The happiness in Stamos' eyes almost made her cry.

"Did you hear him?" Stamos asked in amazement.

"Sure did."

Dillon seemed happy to be the center of attention again. He turned toward Joy and reached for her. "Ma Ma, Ma Ma."

Joy gave Stamos a side-glance. "I'm sure he'll say, Da Da, again real soon."

Stamos laughed. He kissed Dillon's head and Joy's cheek. "I'll be back for lunch."

*****

Joy felt abundantly content as she and Stamos left the doctor's office. It surprised her that Stamos had insisted on taking her. For a brief moment, she didn't want him to go. Her old fear of depending on anyone else came to the surface. Thankfully, a few deep breaths quelled it.

Stamos looked so tall and proud beside her. He took her hand and winked at her, making her blush. His dark hair looked mussed from his fingers going through it the whole time. Joy smiled at him, trying not to laugh.

"What?" Stamos asked, looking puzzled.

"Nothing. Well your hair is a bit..." She burst out laughing, "It's sticking straight up."

Stamos put his Stetson on and gave her a 'so there' look. Reaching for her, Joy was positive he was going to kiss her right in the middle of town. Looking into his eyes, he told her of his love without speaking.

"I was hoping to find you here," Jaime said, stopping before them with Bailey on his arm.

"It's not a good time," Stamos growled.

"Joy, I know you have no reason to trust me, but I need to talk to you. I think I can help," Jamie pleaded.

Joy looked from Stamos to her brother. It could be a set up. "Why don't we talk at Harriet's Tea and Yarn shop?" she suggested, feeling Stamos stiffen next to her.

"Thanks. I'll meet you there in a few. I don't want us seen together."

Joy nodded and they walked away. She took a fortifying breath and turned to hear Stamos out. To her surprise, he looked pleased. "Okay, what's up?" she asked.

"I'm hoping that there is a severe crack in Jaime and Wood's relationship. Maybe cracked enough that we can use it to our advantage."

"If they'd just leave us alone," Joy replied.

"The problem, my love, is that they won't."

Joy nodded as she took Stamos' hand. Smiling at him, she pretended that she hadn't a care in the world while they strolled toward Harriet's shop.

The bell over the door rang out when they entered. The whole room grew silent as the patrons stared. Joy wanted to melt into the wooden floorboards.

There were about five tables all around with different colored tablecloths, dotted around the store. On the walls were shelves and shelves of yarn in brilliant colors. Behind a counter was an area for tea making. It was charming.

Harriett held onto the top of her long black hair as she rushed toward her two new customers. "I'm so glad you decided to visit."

"Thank you," Joy said, feeling awkward. "Maybe we should leave."

"Oh no you don't. Come, I'll introduce you around."

"Actually, Miss Harriett, we're having one of those mood swing type of days. A quiet table with herbal tea and a few tea cakes would be best."

"Of course. Let me get you settled."

Joy smiled at Harriett as she walked past Stamos and kicked his shin. "You'd be surprised that men get the same mood swings. Why, Stamos here was about to cry until I suggested coming in here."

"I've heard of that. You poor dears. I'll have that tea right over for you."

Stamos' eyes narrowed as he held out Joy's chair. "Man mood swings? Really? Why don't you just castrate me?"

Joy laughed hard. Tears ran down her face. "I guess I did play it a bit thick."

"You think? The whole town will know that I'm a teary-eyed cowboy with mood swings."

"I'm sorry." She tried to keep a straight face, but failed miserably.

The bell over the door rang, causing them to let go of all merriment.

Jaime and Bailey walked into the teashop and were quickly blocked from walking any further by Harriett.

"It's all right. I want to talk to him, Harriett," Joy called to her.

Joy couldn't hear, but she thought Harriett growled at the couple. It felt nice to have friends. Jaime looked anxious approaching their table, followed by a very frightened looking Bailey.

"Hi," Jaime greeted, smiling at Joy.

"We are not here for niceties," Stamos warned. "Sit down and say what you want to say then get out."

Jaime's eyes narrowed a bit, but he sat down, nodding to Bailey to do the same.

Joy could see Bailey's annoyance, but she didn't care. "So what did you want to talk about?"

"Dad is trying to kill me," Jaime hissed, as sweat formed on his brow.

"Oh is that all? No big deal, big brother. Just be quicker than your assassin."

Bailey gasped and Jaime's mouth dropped open. "I thought you could help," he whined.

Rage filled Joy's heart upon hearing his words, but when she looked at him all she felt was pity. Their father had duped him. Joy had her suspicions that Jaime knew more than he'd let on, but he'd been young when Daisy had been murdered.

"Why don't you just tell us what's going on?" Stamos asked.

Joy could hear the irritation in his voice and she put her hand on his muscled thigh. He grabbed it and held on.

"Dad upped my life insurance policy. I was almost run down by a car last night. He's out of his mind."

The fear in Jamie's eyes was familiar. Joy had seen the same fear in her own eyes, many times. "Did you report it to the police?"

Jaime's eyes grew wide. "Are you kidding?" he asked, incredulously.

Stamos cleared his throat. "I don't know what you think Joy can do for you, Jaime. She had been fighting to stay alive for nine years. A lot of it has been due to you. I can't wrap my mind around the fact that you threw your sister under the bus."

"She's survived," Jaime whined.

Stamos shook his head, clearly disgusted. "Barely, and she has knife wounds and scars to prove it."

"Are you willing to go to the police?" Joy asked.

Bailey grabbed Jaime's arm. "No. Jaime, he'll kill you for sure. You know it's Joy he wants. We could lay low. We could move."

Jaime looked as though he was going to agree with Bailey and Joy's stomach clenched. Looking around the shop, she noticed that everyone was silent and staring. She couldn't blame them. This was probably the most exciting thing to happen in the teashop in a long time.

"We're done here," Stamos growled.

"Wait," Jaime said his voice in a panic. "I do have some info for you, Joy. Daisy was in on it. She took out the life insurance policy for a million dollars. Dad told her that they would fake her death, and then the two of them could run off leaving you and me behind."

Joy shook her head. "Greed got her killed. I don't feel sorry for her, Dad, or you. Especially not you, Jaime. I took the fall so you wouldn't go to prison. You left me there to rot. You are my big brother. I looked up to you and you never even wrote me a damn letter."

"Joy," Jaime started.

"No. You are on your own just as I was. Watch your back, Jaime. Wood is a sneaky bastard. He'd use Bailey to get to you."

Joy was shaking from her outburst. Was she doing the right thing?

It felt right after all she'd been through. Glancing at Stamos, she could see love and compassion in his eyes. Hell, she'd never have any peace if she didn't help Jaime.

Taking a deep breath, Joy stared hard at Jaime. "We will figure this out together. I have a conscience." Seeing Jaime wince made her feel good. "If you mess with me in any way, I'll cut you loose and Wood is welcome to you."

Jaime looked beaten and contrite. "I'll do anything you say, Joy. I should have had your back in the beginning. I was scared. That's my only defense."

Stamos squeezed her hand lightly and Joy looked at him. Funny how she could read his face. Joy turned toward Jaime and nodded.

"Here is the address of a safe house," Stamos handed Jaime a piece of paper. "Go there. Stay there. Contact no one. A man named Hoss will contact you. Do whatever he says. If you don't follow my rules, we can't help you. And for God's sake don't go home. I'll have Hoss bring you clothes and other necessities. First, drive out of town, make sure no one is following you, and drive to the Whiskey Barrel. Leave your car. A tan station wagon will be parked there."

"A station wagon?" Bailey interrupted.

"Bailey, shut up," Jaime told her, taking the keys from Stamos. "Thank you, both of you."

Joy watched them walk out of The Yarn and Tea Shop, expelling a breath she didn't even realize she was holding. Joy was exhausted. Tears filled her eyes, too many emotions were involved. Somewhere along the way, she'd pushed her feelings about Jaime down into a hidden part of her heart.

Memories of them together as children flooded her mind. She'd followed him everywhere and he didn't seem to mind. A few times his friends complained about having a tagalong and Jaime put them in their place. He'd been her protector, and then he'd been her accuser. The heartache she experienced was overwhelming and she began to sob.

Joy wasn't surprised to find herself on her husband's lap. He enfolded her with his love and she felt safe and cherished. Wiping her tears away with Stamos' clean bandana, Joy became aware that she was the center of attention. How could she have broken down in public? She was losing her edge.

"I'm fine," Joy announced, in a shaky voice and was glad when people turned away.

"Ready to go home?" Stamos asked.

"Always." She took the hand that he offered and they left.

Joy watched out the truck window as the scenery went by. Her mind wasn't on what she was seeing. Anger burned through her veins. It would do no good to drag out and examine her feelings. Joy had the idea she was going to need her edge to survive the next few days. If that meant distancing herself from everyone then so be it.

Her heart clenched as she thought of becoming her old self. The woman that didn't feel. The woman that didn't care. That woman was still alive. She needed to go back to her cold-hearted ways. She wouldn't be able to protect her family if she didn't. She had to get her edge back at all costs.

*****

Stamos looked at his wife for the millionth time that evening. Something was off with her. She shied away from his touch and frankly, it hurt. The more he studied her, the less he knew.

Even little Dillon wasn't the recipient of Joy's loving attention. She let Bea feed him and when he called for her, she left the room.

Naturally she was upset, but she was shutting him out. Stamos had a feeling that Joy was doing it on purpose. Sighing, Stamos looked at her again. Didn't she trust him? Didn't she know that he would keep her safe?

"I'm going to sleep." Joy hastened from the room.

She hadn't even looked at him when she hurried past him. Stamos felt gut-kicked. The way she emphasized sleep let him know that was all they'd be doing in their bed.

He wanted to shake her. He wanted to make her wake up and live her life with him. She'd withdrawn into her shell and he hoped to God he knew what to do to get her back.

The bedroom door was closed. Stamos opened it with a bit of hope that Joy would be waiting for him. Disappointment assailed him. She had her back turned toward him and her eyes closed. He could tell by her breathing that she was not asleep.

Taking his clothes off, he eased under the covers. Reaching for her had been a mistake. The way she shuddered, stiffened, and moved away tore at his heart.

Feeling lost and alone, Stamos stared into the darkness wondering how to fix whatever was wrong. Joy's breathing evened out and he knew she slept.

Stamos tossed and turned, wondering what approach he needed to take. He could confront her, but somehow he knew she'd get her back up and he'd be no better off. What he needed to do was find evidence of her innocence and put her father and brother behind bars. He needed to do it quickly for all of their sakes.

Chapter Thirteen

Joy wiped the sweat off her brow with the sleeve of her shirt. Mucking out stalls was hard work, but that's what she wanted. She needed to keep herself busy and solitary.

The long probing looks that Stamos kept giving her made her want to scream. Everyone had been giving her a wide berth all week. She hadn't heard a word about Jaime and truthfully, she didn't care.

Joy knew that Stamos had had it with her. His tone of voice when he told her to clean the stall was anything but friendly. She hurt him and for that she was sorry. However, in her mind it was unavoidable. The walls around her heart she had put up through her time in prison were back. It was either that or break, and she could never break.

Another shovelful went into the wheelbarrow. It was mindless work. Looking up, her heart stopped, and then it began to beat out of control. At the end of the row of horse stalls, stood her father. He glared at her as he raised his shotgun.

Joy remembered the guns hidden in the wall, but she wasn't near them. Crouching, she ran as fast as she could to the loft ladder. There was a gun hidden in the hollowed out beam. If only she could get there in time.

Almost there. Her calmness was her saving grace. She hit the side of the ladder with great force. Before she could grab the loaded gun, a shot rang out.

Joy grabbed the gun and hit the ground. Everything happened in slow motion. Joy heard a heart-breaking scream as she dived for the floor. Nanny had come out of a stall and was shot. The cries wrenched her heart. Joy aimed the gun at her father. He aimed at her.

He smiled as he brought the shotgun up to his shoulder. Joy rolled away and shot at the same time. He father dropped the rifle, looking shocked. He crumpled to the ground and lay on the dirt floor, unmoving.

Joy immediately got to her feet and ran to Nanny. Oh God, Nanny had stood between her and a bullet. Tears filled her eyes as Nanny continued to scream. Joy prayed that she wouldn't have to put Nanny down.

Kneeling next to the beautiful grey horse, Joy spared a glance at her father. Dead, he was dead. Not giving him another thought, she quickly assessed Nanny's gunshot wound. Crying in relief, Joy shrugged out of her blue shirt and pressed it to Nanny's front flank. The bullet had only grazed her, but there was a lot of blood.

Tears poured down her face. She whispered to Nanny, waiting for help to arrive. She was so intent on Nanny it startled her when a coat settled around her shoulders. She knew from the masculine scent she loved, that it was Stamos.

Leaning back, his arms went around her. Nothing ever felt so good. She glanced at her father and she observed David kneeling over him and then looking at Stamos shaking his head. Joy sensed a laugh trying to bubble within her. She didn't care that she had killed a man. She only cared about Nanny.

"Here, let me keep pressure on her wound," Stamos offered.

"No, don't take your arms away from me. I need to feel you holding me. I'm fine. I want to do this for, Nanny. She saved my life."

"Don't you worry, Joy, I'm not letting you go, ever," Stamos said, huskily.

"She stepped right in front of the bullet, Stamos," Joy whispered.

The smell of blood became overwhelming. Joy's stomach began to roll. "Stamos, I need you to take over."

Stamos gave her a long look and applied pressure to Nanny's wound.

Joy bolted for the door. She barely made it out of the barn before she vomited. It took forever for her stomach to empty. Wobbly, she walked over to the bench and plopped down. Popping a piece of gum in her mouth, she felt the perspiration on her brow. How much was too much?

"Joy, are you all right?" Stamos yelled.

"I'm fine," she yelled back, but she knew that her voice betrayed her tumultuous feelings.

Finally, the police, Ida Perkins, and Doc Parker arrived. The only one Joy was interested in was Doc Parker. She already knew that Nanny would be fine, but she hated that she was in so much pain. Doc Parker could help Nanny with that.

As she watched the police approach her, Joy panicked. She'd never had a good experience with the cops. Having Ida Perkins dogging their heels didn't help any. Joy sat up straight and she narrowed her eyes. "Did you need something?"

"We need to take you in for questioning," one of the police officers told her.

She expected as much. Shrugging, she stood, ready to go. She didn't look anywhere other than the police car. She couldn't. She didn't want to think that it would be her last look. Her fear had come to fruition. She wouldn't be here to watch Dillon grow up. She wouldn't be there to give Stamos his morning and evening kiss. Touching her belly almost made her breakdown.

Sitting in the back of the police car, she told herself to buck up. No whining, no weakness. That hit on her life may still be waiting for her.

The ride was quick and as the car parked, Joy caught site of Ida smiling at her. She tried to ignore her, but Ida made it impossible. Joy wanted to smack her when she insisted on being in the interrogation room. Somehow, Ida got her way and they all went inside together.

The interrogation room was standard. It had the two-way mirror, the camera, and stiff uncomfortable chairs. Hers rocked a bit and she had to bite back a smile. She knew that it was a tactic to keep the prisoner unsteady and miserable.

The brick walls were painted the same ugly green as all the rest and she wanted to laugh as it grew warmer in the room. Textbook, that's what it was. Didn't they know that she was a hardened convict and she was on to their tactics?

They offered her coffee, which she refused. One time she drank several sodas and then they wouldn't allow her to use the bathroom. Adding Ida to the mix might even be fun. Good cop, bad cop, and evil witch. That combo she'd never had.

The door opened and the three of them walked in. Joy bit her lip and looked away. Taking a deep steadying breath, she sat back in the chair and stared defiantly at them.

"Why don't we begin with how you killed your father?" Ida asked, almost gleefully.

Joy ignored her. It was either that or go over the table and strangle her. Shifting so that she looked in the direction of the police, Joy waited.

The two officers looked at each other. It was obvious they didn't work out who was good cop and who was bad. Amateur hour, but she had to endure it.

Officer Rice, the bigger of the two with curly blond hair and piercing blue eyes, cleared his throat. "We have the murder weapon, a dead body, and you."

The other one, Officer Terrell smiled at her. "Now, I'm sure that you have a good explanation. You didn't mean to kill your father, did you?" He played with his handlebar mustache.

They both stared at her waiting for a confession.

"Oh please," Ida said with disgust. "She killed her father. We have the evidence, we don't need a confession."

Officer Rice threw her a dirty look. "We need to hear your statement."

Officer Terrell smiled. "It's the fastest way to get out of here."

Joy snorted. "Are you offering me a get out of jail free card? If not, then I want a lawyer."

"Oh, come on, don't go and lawyer up. That is the stupidest thing I've ever heard." Officer Rice pounded the table with his fist.

"Y'all can pound that table all you want. This is not my first rodeo. I want a lawyer."

She smiled as they all looked at each other. They were out of gas.

Except for Ida, she jumped out of her chair and grabbed Joy by her long braid. Putting her face right in front of Joy's, Ida hissed, "Oh no, you are not getting out of it this time. You killed your father and your stepmother. You are a monster and I won't rest until you are behind bars."

The pain of having her hair pulled was immense, but Joy barely flickered an eyelash. Ida wanted to get a rise out of her and Joy did not intend to cooperate.

"Let go, Miss Perkins." Officer Terrell stood up, walked around the table, and tried to pry Ida's hand open.

It wasn't until Officer Rice got up that Ida paid any mind to what they were saying. Finally, she let go of Joy's hair and the three exited the room, but not before Ida gave her a long vicious look.

Joy looked at the two-way mirror and resisted the urge to smile. She knew they were all behind it talking about her and watching her. Her nightmares never ceased.

Somehow, she thought that Stamos would have called her a lawyer by now. Unless he didn't believe it was self-defense. Maybe he agreed with witch Perkins. Taking a deep breath, Joy knew no matter what, Stamos would always be there for her. That's what love meant.

He'd be there and soon. She would just have to wait a little bit longer. But as the hours passed, Joy grew less and less confident.

Her warring heart drew her into deep misery. He loves me, he loves me not. Her mind whirled and whirled until she didn't know which way was up. So many untruths in her life, how was she to know what was real and what was just plain made up?

Shaking her head, she thought of Dillon. That was a true love. The bliss she experienced when he was in her arms was genuine. Next, she thought of Stamos. That was a true love wasn't it? Their lovemaking had been just that, making love. Hadn't it?

Putting her hand over her abdomen, she knew that the love for her baby was real. The whole world around her had been so crazy, so full of betrayal and deceit that Joy felt bereft.

She didn't even know who she was. Was she the hardened women who refused to lower her guard? Was she the warm and loving wife and mother? Was she the respected friend or was that all an illusion too?

Maybe she'd been a fool to believe in Stamos. Her heart was being squeezed in her chest. Breathing became hard and she washed herself in despair. Where was he?

She sat with her back toward the mirror. Not so others couldn't see her. She didn't want to see herself. She couldn't face herself if she'd been a fool. Five long hours she'd been sitting alone. As she waited, her faith waned and her mind tortured her with doubt.

Fear found its way inside her and try as she might she couldn't push it out. She should have stayed in prison in the first place. Her life would have been better if she'd never gone to Stamos' ranch. Then she thought of her unborn baby and knew that she couldn't regret it.

Was this purgatory or was it hell? Having been happy made her situation even harder to bear. She couldn't take any more and the tears that had been waiting to fall, trailed down her face. This time she didn't try to stop them. What was the use? There was no one to see them. No one for her to draw comfort from. She felt reminiscent of that scared fourteen-year-old girl that had first been put in prison. She was on her own, once again. It was official, she'd been born under an unlucky star.

The door handle turned and Joy anxiously waited to see who'd come through it.

"Joy, are you okay?" Callie asked as she approached Joy.

Joy gave her a weak smile. Her heart hurt. She had expected Stamos to be the one who came. "Yes, of course I am. This is nothing new to me."

Callie took her hand and pulled her up. "Let's get out of here."

Joy stood open mouthed. "I can go?"

Callie smiled at her. "Yes and we need to get out of here before these jackasses change their minds."

Joy nodded and allowed Callie to lead her out of the interrogation room. She wanted to turn and stick her tongue out at the two-way mirror, but she resisted the urge. All she wanted was to go home.

She blinked at the bright sun while she walked to Callie's truck. Where was Stamos? Joy was too proud to ask her friend where he was. It killed her not asking, but she had her pride.

Joy waited in vain for Callie to tell her what was going on. She listened while Callie talked about Garrett and her twins. She half listened and hoped that she was making the right responses. Her mind was too full of questions for her to give Callie her full attention.

Joy watched in horror as Callie passed the turnoff to her ranch. She wasn't going home after all. Stamos probably didn't want her around Dillon. She was a killer now. It was real this time.

"Almost there," Callie announced cheerfully.

Joy nodded, biting her lip until she tasted blood. This was too much. All this turmoil couldn't be good for the baby. Taking a deep breath, Joy tried to grin and bear it. Unfortunately, it didn't take away the excruciating pain in her heart. That, she knew, was permanent.

Callie parked the truck and they both quickly got out. No one came out to greet them and Joy's last tiny bit of hope faded. She supposed that this was where she'd be staying for a while. At least she was with friends.

"I'm going to the barn," Joy called out, as she headed in the opposite direction of Callie. She needed to be alone for a bit.

Walking into the big barn made her smile. The smell of horses and hay brought down her anxiety level. Nino, Nanny's foal, greeted her. "Hey, girl. How's your mom?"

Nino put her head over Joy's shoulder, hugging her. Joy closed her eyes and enjoyed the moment. When she opened them, she was surprised to see both Garret and Stamos. "Oh."

Taking a step back from the horse, Joy nodded at both men. "How is Nanny?" she asked, looking only at Stamos. He was a welcome sight and she needed to drink in his essence.

"She'll be fine." Garrett walked past Joy, patting her on the shoulder.

Stamos stared back at her. It was impossible to know what he was thinking. He looked so solemn.

"Will you be bringing my things over or have you already done it?" Joy asked, miserably.

"Your things?" Stamos asked, taking a step toward her.

"Yes."

"What are you talking about? Are you all right?" Stamos asked, taking another step in her direction.

Joy nodded. "I'm fine. I realize that you don't want me around Dillon anymore and..."

Stamos took another step until he stood in front of Joy. "Joy, what in God's name is going on in that mind of yours?"

Joy felt as confused as Stamos looked. "I figured since you didn't come to get me, and I'm here instead of at home..."

Stamos cradled her cheek in the palm of his hand. "Oh, Joy. I'm sorry. I should have been the one to get you. I was here helping with Nanny and Callie offered to go and get you. It never occurred to me that you'd think there was something wrong. Dillon and I have been crazy all day without you."

Joy looked into his eyes and knew that he was telling the truth. Pulling away, she turned her back to him. "I-- I just don't know what to think, what to feel. I'm afraid, Stamos, so afraid. My doubts have shredded all of my faith and confidence in us. I can't seem to rid myself of a feeling of doom. A feeling that I'm headed for destruction."

Joy's voice quavered and it made her mad. "I've turned into a weak ninny here at your ranch. I have wants and desires that I can't have. Not anymore."

Stamos stepped behind her and she pulled away. "No, don't touch me." Turning, she glimpsed the hurt in his eyes. It made her heart twist painfully. "What would have happened if they'd locked me up? My mind can't seem to get rid of you, Dillon, and the ranch. You are all I think about and that could get me killed. It could get our baby killed. Stamos, the world is a dangerous place and prison is a hundred times so."

Stamos nodded. He looked as though he understood. He didn't look happy, but he got it. "You owe me..."

"Stamos, don't be that way," Joy pleaded.

"You owe me a good morning kiss. A promise is a promise," he told her with a stubborn look on his face.

"Stamos..."

"No you listen to me for a change. I understand where you are coming from. You are right if you were going to prison, but you're not."

"But--"

Stamos held up his hand to stay her. "It's my turn. I love you with everything I have; everything I am. My son loves you. You are his mother. The baby you carry is a part of both of us. Do you think I wanted to let you into my heart? No, I did not. I've been hurt in my life too." Stamos took a deep breath. "Here's the thing, only you can decide to be a part of this family. You still have to stay until your prison work release is done. Let me know what you decide."

Stamos stepped forward and grabbed her hips, hauling her against him. He slanted his lips over hers, plundering her mouth. He kissed her long and hard, making her gasp. Then just as suddenly, he put her from him and walked away, leaving her feeling bereft.

Joy walked to the stall where Nanny was recuperating. She looked good. Opening the stall door, she went inside and knelt down to stroke Nanny's head. The vet must have given her a sedative, but Joy knew that Nanny was aware of her presence.

"Thank you, Nanny, you saved my life." Joy sighed. "My life, what a mess. Nanny, I just don't know what to do. My heart says one thing but my head says another. I love that man of mine with my heart and soul. Why can't I get past all the warnings in my head?"

Nanny looked at her and nickered.

"You're right. Life is too short."

The stall door opened and in came Pirate, the love of Nanny's life. Right behind him was their daughter Nino. Joy leaned down and kissed Nanny on her head. "I understand now. Thank you."

*****

Stamos looked up from his desk. He knew it was Joy and Dillon. He just wasn't in the mood for either. He felt bordering on an injured bull and he didn't want to take out his anger on either of them.

Joy continued to stand there. Stamos wished her away to no avail. He did notice in the brief look he gave them, that Joy had let her hair down. Did she know that it made him crazy? Probably she was using it as a weapon against his resolve to stay angry. Looking up at her again, he noticed the sorrow in her eyes. He looked away. She was using every female trick to get to him.

"Okay, you can go now," he said, without looking up.

Joy gasped, but she didn't leave.

"What do you want, Joy? And let me warn you I'm not in the mood for any nonsense."

"Nonsense? How dare you," Joy cried.

Stamos stared at her and smiled. "Oh I dare, sweetheart. I dare a lot."

"No. We are not going to do this," Joy told him.

"Not with Dillon in the room anyway." Stamos shrugged. "If you want to come back later, well, we'll see."

He could see the hurt and confusion in Joy's eyes before she turned and fled. Hell. He hadn't planned to act that way. He lashed out at her because he hurt. Why was it that every time they were almost there on their way to happiness, something grabbed it away?

This time that something was him. He needed space. He needed time. He needed to ride the range on Frankie. Stamos' lips twitched. Joy had him calling Franklin, Frankie. She'd love to know that. Maybe when he got back.

Walking to the barn, Stamos pulled his hat down further on his head. A cold wind blew across the Texas grass. "What are you doing in here and why is my son out in the cold?"

Joy flinched at his harsh words. "I'm so sorry. I will bring *your* son back inside." She brushed past him.

Corny, Rowdy, and Shep all stared at him with their mouths hanging open. "Get to work," Stamos, growled. It didn't give him any satisfaction to see them scramble.

Saddling Frankie, Stamos thought about Joy. Maybe she was trying to make amends. Hell. She hadn't done anything. "Hey, Corny I've changed my mind. Could you unsaddle Frankie for me?"

Corny took the reins smiling at Stamos the whole time. The whole ranch was loco. Stamos pushed his hat back and strode toward the house. He wanted to be with his wife and their son.

The house seemed uncharacteristically quiet. Stamos wondered where everyone was. Pouring himself a cup of coffee, he thought maybe he heard someone in his office. He grabbed his cup and peered into the room. It was Joy.

Standing with her back to him, she looked out the window. It was obvious that she was crying, and Stamos knew how much she hated to cry. Her hair hung down her back like a shiny curtain of brown and gold. She had filled out in all the right places. Her ass looked wonderful.

He could feel himself harden. His whole body ignited in anticipation. He wanted her more than he had ever wanted anyone. She was his woman and it was time she knew it.

Joy stood at the window trembling. Her head turned slightly as Stamos approached. She didn't turn around.

Stamos sighed, and then he moved directly behind her. He wrapped one arm around her middle as he kissed her up and down the side of her neck. He could feel her shiver with each kiss.

"Stamos," she moaned.

It was all the encouragement he needed. He hastily unbuttoned her shirt and pulled her bra down, exposing her soft breasts. He found both nipples and rolled them between his fingers. They were heavier and by her throaty moans, he could tell they were more sensitive too.

Joy began to rub her ass against him. It was both pure heaven and torture, he wanted it to last. He reached down, unbuttoned her jeans, and removed both her jeans and her sexy black lace panties.

He moved her away from the window and had her facing the wall. "Hold on to the wall baby, this is going to be a wild ride."

Joy laughed, but did as he asked.

Undressing, he looked at her magnificent ass. "You are one sexy woman."

Joy turned her head and looked at him as though he was crazy. "If you say so."

Stamos came up behind her, rubbing against her. "I know so." He reached around her and grabbed her breasts again. Reaching down he could feel her readiness and he entered her.

"Oh, Stamos. Oh God. Faster. Faster," Joy cried out, arching her back as she came.

Stamos drove into her once, twice, three times before he shuddered. He was surprised to feel her shuddering around him again. It felt magical.

They stood there for a few minutes until they both caught their breath. Stamos took a step back and as Joy turned around, he scooped her up in his arms and kissed her deeply.

Her eyes were wide with wonder. "Wow. Does that mean you're not mad at me?"

Stamos sat on the couch with Joy still in his arms. He grabbed the plaid blanket off the back of the couch and covered them both. Joy's squirming was starting to make him crazy. Finally, she settled against him.

"Joy I'm so sorry."

*****

They sat there together for a while, both quiet.

Joy gazed into the dark liquid pools that were his eyes. The truth of his statement shined through. Reaching up, she ran her hand along his chin, unshaven and strong. It made him look sexy.

Her breath caught as he hardened under her. She could feel it strong and throbbing against her bare skin. Turning, she faced Stamos with her legs straddled on both sides of him. Joy reached down to touch that hardness.

The silky softness of it was such a contrast to its throbbing hardness. Smiling she looked at Stamos, whose eyes were closed. A deep throaty moan of pleasure escaped his lips as she moved her hand along the thick hardness. Joy knew a woman's power when it hardened even more.

Stamos leaned down and took one of her strawberry red nipples into his mouth, sucking on it. Joy jumped at the jolt of electricity that burst throughout her whole body. Heat pooled in her lower region and she needed him.

"Stamos, please," she begged.

Stamos looked at her and smiled. Lifting her, he settled her over him, and thrust into her.

Joy gasped at the suddenness of taking him all in. She struggled for breath as Stamos put his big, strong hands on her rear-end and guided her up and down. The fullness was incredible. Joy wanted it to last forever.

Looking down, she could see them joined and that put her over the edge. She cried out, convulsing around him. Joy heard him cry and stiffen inside her.

Joy stayed where she was, with Stamos inside of her. Putting her arms around his neck, she drew him close to her. Laying her cheek on his shoulder, she experienced such closeness to Stamos.

Joy started to pull away only to have Stamos hold her close to him. It made her feel loved, special, and very sexy. She'd been a fool, time and time again, pushing him away.

Chapter Fourteen

Joy watched the sunrise, holding Dillon, rocking him back and forth. Today her father was to be laid to rest. Part of her mourned for the little girl inside of her that had loved and trusted her father. She really thought he'd hung the moon. Joy also mourned her innocent soul, scarred by her father's deceit.

"Dillon, you don't know how lucky you are to have a man like your daddy in your life." Kissing his forehead, she continued. "He's a decent, loving, honest man."

"That you love to pieces," Stamos said, from the doorway, causing Joy to turn.

"You scared me," Joy said smiling. "I do, you know, love you to pieces."

"Who couldn't love me? I have all my teeth and I own horses and..."

Joy laughed, loving the sight of him. His hair was rumpled and he had a light beard. He was one sexy man. He only wore low-slung jeans with the button undone. The muscles in his chest and abs made her stomach flutter. Just remembering last night, being in his strong arms, made her blush.

Stamos smiled a slow sexy smile. "It's the teeth, I can tell. That's why you love me."

"Yes you are right. I love that you have your teeth. Now go get dressed while I get your son dressed."

Stamos approached them and kissed Joy's cheek. "Our son. I'm so sorry I said he wasn't. It will never happen again. I promise."

Joy looked at him and her eyes teared up. "Thank you," she whispered.

"It's Dillon and I that are the lucky ones. Right Dill?"

Dillon reached out and grabbed Stamos' hair, laughing all the while.

Joy handed Dillon over to his father, laughing herself. "I'm going to get dressed while you two work this out."

"Payback, Joy," Stamos said, in a very suggestive voice.

"You can pay me back around noon, cowboy," Joy said as she left, hearing Stamos first laugh, then talking to Dillon, encouraging him to let go of his hair.

Yes, she was the lucky one. She was safe and well loved, if last night was any indication. Joy smiled as she thought of their lovemaking. Stamos was insatiable and she hadn't minded one bit. Things were just going to get better and better.

*****

To Joy's great disappointment, their noon date didn't happen. Instead, she looked out the front window, watching her brother drive up. What he wanted she couldn't imagine. She hoped he didn't think they'd be a family again. The thought disgusted her.

The look of rage on Jaime's face worried Joy. He stalked to the door and pounded on the door. Taking a deep breath Joy opened the door.

Red-faced, Jaime pushed past Joy. It surprised her but she could take care of herself. The look of fury on his face, she hadn't seen before.

"What is it now?"

"As if you didn't know, you bitch."

Joy watched Jaime clench and unclench his fists. She was concerned that he meant to hit her. Out of the corner of her eyes, she saw Bea peek into the room. Bea nodded and left.

"Jaime, I'm not in the mood for your games."

"How'd you do it, Joy? Was I put into protective custody so you could get on father's good side?" he yelled.

Joy shook her head. "Father didn't have a good side, Jaime. You know that. I wouldn't have gone near him with a ten-foot pole."

"You are cut from the same skin -- skunk skin. You lured him here to kill him. If it hadn't been so diabolically sneaky, costing me everything, I would have applauded you. Now I have no choice. I have to kill you and that meddling husband of yours."

Joy put her hand to her throat as she drew in a sharp breath. "I have no idea what you're talking about. How dare you come to my house and threaten my family."

Jaime grabbed her by the shoulders and shoved her hard against the wall. "You are going to give me the money you stole or the Walker clan will be dead."

Joy rubbed the back of her head, trying to figure out what to do. If she weren't pregnant, she would have jumped him and fought back. "Jaime, you can have the money. Just tell me where it is," Joy said, in a dead calm voice.

"Don't play coy with me, little sister. You snuggled up to father and had him change his will and his life insurance. You get everything."

"And I believe that is a motive for murder," Ida Perkins accused as she walked into the house. Her mousey brown hair was pulled back so drastically it gave her a look of a gargoyle.

Joy gasped looking at the other woman. Ida shot Jaime a smile of adoration while she pulled out her gun. "We'll make her pay, Jaime. The justice system won't punish her."

Jaime seemed genuinely surprised to see Ida. He quickly went to her side, sneering at Joy. "That's right, she needs to be punished."

Ida gave him a wide smile. "She hasn't finished paying for killing Daisy, but she will."

Jaime laughed loud and hard. "Funny thing, she didn't kill Daisy. I did."

A loud gasp came from the doorway causing everyone to turn. There stood Bailey, her eyes blazing. Her face grew red and her mouth contorted. "You lied to me. You said that Joy killed your stepmother," she screeched. "I believed you. I love you. How can you make me the fool?"

Jaime took a step toward her. "Now, honey, you know that all I want is the best for us."

Ida laughed. "Oh give it up, Jaime. You might as well tell this little tart that you've been using her. Tell her that she is indeed a fool. The biggest fool of all." Ida smiled at Bailey as she put her arm through Jaime's and pressed herself against him. "Listen, honey, men don't always tell the truth. Jaime lied to me, but we love each other. We have for over ten years. That's right, I knew Jaime before Daisy was even killed. Daisy was my sister."

Joy didn't know what to think. She never heard that Daisy even had a sister. At this point, she didn't much care who tricked whom. She needed to get out of there. Taking one-step back, waiting, then another, Joy inched away. If she turned and ran, she might be able to reach the front door before they caught her.

Bailey provided the distraction by launching herself at Ida, kicking and biting. The screaming between the two was loud. Joy didn't stay to watch. She turned and fled. Sailing out the door, she didn't even look back. If they were going to kill her then they'd have to shoot her in the back.

She ran toward the barn. Hopefully she'd be able to grab a rifle there again. She was almost there when she was suddenly blocked from entering. Long arms grabbed her and hauled her into the barn. Joy was momentarily stunned and her whole body began to shake.

Taking a deep breath, Joy sighed in relief as she smelled leather, horses, and balsam. "Where's Dillon?" she asked, turning around.

Stamos stepped back and looked Joy over. "He's off the ranch with Bea. I told her to take him to Callie's house."

"She made it," Garrett told them as he entered the back of the barn.

"Good to have you here, Garrett," Stamos said seriously.

"So what's going on?" Garrett asked. Both men looked at Joy.

"Jaime, Ida, and Bailey are all in the house. They'll be right behind me any time now. They plan to kill me, Stamos, and Dillon. My father left everything to me when he died and Jaime thinks if he wipes us out it goes to him."

"No offense, but your family is loco," Garret said in disgust.

"Believe me, I know." Joy grabbed a rifle from Stamos.

"Up to the loft with you," Stamos told her, kissing her forehead.

"But--"

"No, I need to know that you're safe. I can't have a clear head if I'm worrying about you."

Joy gave him a long measured look. She nodded and scurried up the ladder. Once again, she'd brought danger to this ranch. She felt sick to her stomach. Lying down behind a few bales of hay, she could still see most of the barn. She'd have their backs if it came to it.

A shot rang out. It came from the house. Joy wondered which one of the three was shot. It didn't really matter. Bailey deserved it the least. Jamie really did trick her.

Loud voices could be heard, then silence. It was a chilly day, yet Joy could feel sweat on her brow. The echo of the door slamming got her attention. They were coming.

Joy looked down and spotted both Stamos and Garrett hiding in the horses' stalls. Looking further, she became aware of Corny, Arlo, and Shep, all armed and waiting. It was a relief to have backup.

Jaime came running in, the wild look in his eyes disturbed her. He looked as insane as her father did. Ida came in breathing heavily right behind him. Both looked around frantically.

"We have to find her before Stamos gets home," Jaime told Ida.

"Well, don't kill her until we know where the little brat is. Then we'll take the truck and run Stamos down. I always wanted to shoot someone out of their saddle," Ida said, laughing.

"Shhh, we need to find that vengeful bitch."

Joy watched them slowly walk toward the stalls. Ida started sneezing. Hay fever, Joy mused. Jaime did not look happy about it at all. From the look he gave Ida, Joy figured she'd be dead before sunset.

"Okay, Joy, just come out and we can talk about this whole thing. No one has to get hurt. I just need your signature," Jaime cajoled as he continued to inch forward.

"Oh for heavens sake. Get your ass out here or we will torture Stamos before we kill him," Ida yelled.

"She's not here," Corny yelled from the last stall.

"Bull," Jaime yelled, aiming his gun. He only got one shot off before Stamos leaped out and tackled him.

Garrett grabbed Ida, who was kicking and screaming.

Joy watched in horror as Jaime waved the gun around. Stamos and Jaime rolled once, twice, while Stamos tried to gain control of the pistol. A shot rang out, then a scream.

"You shot me," Ida said in disbelief as she clutched her chest.

Garrett immediately put her on her back and pressed hard on her wound, trying to staunch the blood. Jaime dropped the gun. All fight seemed to go out of him as he crawled toward Ida.

As soon as Stamos had possession of the gun, Joy climbed down from the loft and hugged him tight. His shoulders were broad and he'd had the weight of her problems on them. She hoped that now that burden would be considerably lightened.

"Ida, don't die. Please don't die," Jaime begged, with tears in his eyes. He grabbed her hand and held strong.

"Jaime, Jaime, I love you. It was always you. None of this is your fault. Daisy was the evil one, not us. She shouldn't have seduced you. She shouldn't have taken you away from me."

Joy watched in confusion. What the hell was going on? Jaime and Daisy were sleeping together? Nothing made sense anymore. Everything she knew to be true, wasn't. It threw her balance off. Leaning against Stamos, she realized that being off balance wasn't such a bad thing if she had the right person to lean on. It scared her, but she was learning.

The death rattle that came from Ida was startling. There was an awful gurgling sound, and then nothing.

Garrett looked their way and shook his head.

Jaime took Ida in his arms and cried. Joy almost felt sorry for him, almost. It was a great relief when the authorities arrived and carted him off. Finally, the right person would be behind bars.

Joy stood back and watched as Stamos walked Garrett to his truck. They shook hands before Garrett took off. Joy walked over to her husband, taking his hand.

"Talk about a heck of a day," Stamos said, giving her hand a squeeze.

"I'm worn out," Joy commented.

"Come on, I'll put you to bed," Stamos said, scooping her up into his arms.

"You don't need to carry me," she protested.

"I don't want you too tired."

"Why?"

"I thought maybe you'd want to spend some time with, *The Stamos*," Stamos said, giving her a slow sexy smile.

Joy felt her face grow warm. "You know how much I love *The Stamos*."

Joy wriggled out of his grasp. He put her down. "What's wrong?"

"What about Bailey? I can't go in that house," Joy stammered, turning white.

Stamos led her to the porch swing, he helped her sit. "I'll go in and find out what's going on. I'm sorry, I was just so relieved that you weren't hurt that I wasn't thinking."

Joy gave him a shy smile. "For a moment there cowboy, neither was I."

*****

Stamos kissed the top of her head, and then headed into the house. His gut clenched when he smelled the metallic tang of blood. A police officer put up his hand signaling for Stamos to stop.

"What's going on? Is she... Is she dead?"

"No, it's a shoulder wound. Guess she played dead. Bailey is smarter than I ever gave her credit for," the young officer said.

Stamos nodded. "So she's going to be all right?"

"Looks like it. The house and barn are crime scenes. The sheriff wants everyone downtown to give statements."

If it hadn't been so serious, Stamos might have smiled at the officer's last comment. Downtown Lasso Springs was a one-stoplight town. "I'll round everyone up."

"Thanks. I'm sure that after we get the statements you can come back to the ranch. I have to warn you, there's a lot of blood in the study. It ain't a pretty sight."

Stamos sighed as he ran his fingers through his hair. "Well, thanks for that. Joy is pregnant and I'd hate for her to see it."

Stamos walked outside and looked at Joy. His fierce, brave, wonderful, wife. His heart overflowed with the love he held for that spitfire of a woman. She'd been a hard nut to crack, but it had been worth it. He wasn't so sure in the beginning. He'd thought that maybe she'd been in prison too long and she'd grown too tough.

He smiled realizing that it had taken some doing, but he'd gotten past all the tough prison mentality. Inside he'd found the most wonderful treasure. He'd found Joy.

Chapter Fifteen

Looking at Stamos' profile made Joy feel tranquil. She'd never experienced such peace. The car heater blasted as Johnny Cash's voice filled the truck. They'd given their statements to the police and to Joy's surprise they allowed her to walk away.

Stamos' black whiskers were growing in heavy on his strong jaw line. He looked both tired and sexy. From the moment they got into the truck, he'd entwined his fingers with hers, not letting go. His hand looked bigger than hers did, but Joy knew they were both equally as strong.

"I can't wait to curl up in bed with you," Joy said.

"We can't go home, honey. The place is a mess and it's a crime scene."

Joy's shoulder's sagged in disappointment.

"Don't worry honey, we're going to Callie and Garrett's. Bea and Dillon are there. We'll spend the night and take it from there."

Joy smiled at Stamos. "Keep your eyes on the road buddy," she teased.

"I like the view inside better." He flashed her one of his sexy grins.

"Me too," Joy said quietly.

The anticipation of seeing Dillon filled her. Joy scrambled out of the truck as soon as it stopped and hurried past Stamos toward the front door.

"I was going to help you down."

"I want to see my son," Joy told him, knocking on the door.

Garrett opened the door, took one look at Joy, and pointed to the family room. Joy brushed past him, taking off her gloves, hat, and coat in record speed.

She stopped when she spotted Callie rocking Dillon, with a look of joy on her face. Callie extended her arms, giving Dillon to Joy.

A wave of love rushed through her as she held Dillon in her arms. His eyes opened and he smiled a toothless grin. Joy's heart melted. "Ma Ma," he cried in glee.

A single tear escaped and trailed down her face. The horror of the day came pouring back, making Joy realize that because of her, Dillon had been in danger. Joy handed Dillon back to Callie. "Where?"

"Your room is the last door on the right," Callie told her.

Joy nodded her thanks and ran from the room, up the stairs and into her bedroom. She paced back and forth and then she suddenly ran to the bathroom where she got sick.

Rinsing her mouth, Joy looked at herself in the mirror. Once bad

Lone Star Joy

luck, always bad luck. Her stomach still rebelled. Grabbing the tissues, Joy sat on the cold tile floor. She leaned against the wall, trying to staunch the continuous flow of tears. She was unsuccessful, which only made her cry harder.

She wasn't surprised when Stamos entered the room. Joy tried to smile, but failed.

Stamos helped her up from the floor and drew her into his arms. "Demons?"

Joy nodded her head, and then rested it on his muscular chest. Wrapping her arms around him, she held on tight. "I can't escape them."

"Shhh, I'm here. I'll help to keep them at bay," Stamos told her, kissing her wet cheek.

Joy liked the thought of keeping them at bay. Only Stamos would understand that she couldn't vanquish them completely. Not after the hell she'd been through. "I still feel shocked at Jaime and Ida's confessions. It makes me sick to think about it."

"I know, me too," Stamos assured her. He pulled her down on the bed. Tucking her head under his, against his shoulder, he rubbed her back.

"I still can't make sense of it all. They were all sick, all four of them, my father, Jaime, Daisy, and Ida."

"Yeah, I have to admit the whole Ida thing took me by surprise. I knew she had it in for you, but I had no idea she'd been involved."

Joy sighed and snuggled against Stamos' side. "Oh," she said, surprised. Lifting her head, she stared into Stamos' dark eyes. "I can feel the baby move."

Stamos smiled, put his hand on her abdomen and held it there.

Joy was amazed at how his hand covered her whole midsection. It felt amazingly intimate to have him touching her there, waiting for the baby to move. "Boy or girl?"

"Hell, I don't care. Kids are kids. You just love them whatever they are."

Tears streamed down her face, and Stamos looked concerned.

"What? Did I say something wrong?" he asked.

"No, you big hearted man. It's your beautiful words making me cry. I love you. All those years of loneliness brought me to you. I doubted it for a long time, but now I believe that there is a God."

Running her fingers over his face, Joy could feel his strength, not just physical strength, but inner strength. "I feel as though my heart has been in a vise for so long. You set it free. I don't feel the need to sit with my back to the wall or be on guard at all times."

Stamos took her hand in his and kissed her fingers.

"I have George to thank for believing in me. I'd been alone for so long that I really didn't believe he meant to help me. I figured there would be a price."

"There are good people in this world." Stamos kissed her palm, making her shiver.

"I know that now. I have a husband, a son, a baby on the way, friends..." Joy sniffled, shaking her head. "I'm amazed. I spent day after day, year after year alone. Totally alone. It's hard to fathom that I've been given such gifts."

"You know what?"

"What?" Joy asked.

"You talk too much, woman." Stamos kissed the side of her neck, causing her to giggle.

"I just giggled. Now I know I've gone off the deep end."

"Music to my ears," Stamos said, grinning at her. "Want to fool around?"

Joy pulled his head down, kissing him deeply, lovingly. "Uh oh," she said pushing him away. "Your baby is making me sick." Joy jumped off the bed and ran for the bathroom.

"How come it's my baby when you're sick?" Stamos yelled out, teasing her.

*****

Stamos sat at the kitchen table trying to entertain all three children, while Callie was upstairs with Joy. He wanted to be the one to help, but Callie pushed him out of the way and walked into the bathroom, shutting the door in his face. "Go watch the children," she had yelled through the door.

Rose was drinking milk and making it come out her nose. Dillon laughed while Aidan started throwing cereal on the floor.

"Stamos, weren't you watching them?" Callie asked, standing over him with her hands on her hips.

"Yes."

"Well?"

"I don't get why you're mad."

"Men. I just don't understand you. Just who do you think has to clean all this mess up?" she demanded, her eyes full of humor.

"You?"

"No way, cowboy." She laughed, handing him the broom. "Start with the cereal."

Joy when she spotted him. "I don't think I've ever seen you with a broom before."

"It's not a sight to get used to," he warned.

"Good lord, sit down Joy," Callie demanded.

"I'm fine."

Stamos tried not to laugh, but he couldn't help himself. "Better do as she says or it's housework for you."

Stamos' heart grew, watching her smile. That was all he wanted to do for the rest of his life. He wanted Joy to smile.

*****

Three days later, they were driving home. It surprised her that Callie hadn't been there to say goodbye. Luckily, Joy had thanked her for her hospitality the night before.

It wasn't a far drive and Joy was filled with a sense of excitement and dread. She wanted to be home with her family, but knowing that Bailey had been shot in the house and Ida in the barn, was in the back of her mind. Glancing at Stamos, she felt safe. He was her rock, the one that kept her sane.

They were almost to the turnoff and Joy thought about all the blood that must be in the house. "Will Bea be coming home today or tomorrow?"

"You know, I forgot to ask. She seems to be having a great visit with her sister."

Joy nodded absently. Well first she'd get the blood off the floor. Then her thoughts drifted as car after car came into view. Someone at the ranch was having a party. Oh no, she didn't want any of the men to get into trouble over it.

Joy looked at Stamos, waiting for his frown, but it never happened. Something strange was going on and she just didn't have the emotional energy to ask what. They must have invited women too, she mused, noticing that not all the vehicles were pickups.

Stamos parked the truck and winked at Joy. "I know you're tired, my love, but the good folks of Lasso Springs wanted to make sure the house was clean for our return."

Joy smiled and kissed his cheek. "Well, cowboy, let's go greet our friends." Joy bounded out of the truck and reached for Dillon's car seat. It took a lot of practice to get him in and out of the contraption, but she finally got it down.

Stamos put his arms around her shoulder, guiding them all toward the house. It puzzled Joy that no one had come out to greet them.

Walking into the house, Joy held her breath. She hoped the coppery smell of blood was gone. Tears filled her eyes at the sight of the blue and pink decorations. A baby shower. Joy looked questioning at Stamos.

"Yes it's for you and the baby."

"Wow."

"Well finally. Everyone, the guests of honor are here," Harriett announced, her voice shrill and her long black wig off center.

"Where is my Bobby?" Mable asked as she hurried toward the couple and edged her way in front of Harriett, giving her a dirty look. "My Bobby is the most important person here. He should greet the guests of honor first."

"Don't you start with me, Mable. I own my own business. I'm important," Harriet yelled, indignantly.

"Ladies you're scaring Dillon," Stamos told them.

They both stopped and made silent Os with their mouths.

"Just look at him, Mable, isn't he cute?" Harriet asked.

"Almost as cute as my Bobby," Mable answered.

Callie came rushing toward the group. "Hells bells, there you are. Come on, we have presents to open and cake to eat."

Stamos took a step back. "Well, if you ladies will excuse me, I'll let you have your little hen party."

Callie laughed. "Not a chance, this is one of those him and her baby showers."

Joy almost laughed at the surprise on Stamos' face. "Come on, cowboy, let's join the party."

*****

Looking up at the Texas sky, Joy felt tempted to try to jump and grab the moon. It looked so huge and illuminated. She didn't need the moon. She loved the man who hung the moon, at least for her. Autumn was in full force. The colors of the leaves were a kaleidoscope of reds, yellows, and oranges. A Texas breeze shook the leaves, making them sound like rain.

Taking a deep breath of the cool crisp air, Joy was thankful. George had told her that he had been working on her behalf to clear her name. He was optimistic that it would be before Christmas. What a present that would be, she mused.

The front door opened and closed, Joy didn't have to turn around to know it was Stamos. He walked up behind her, put his arms around her middle, and kissed her neck causing her to shiver.

"What are you thinking about?"

"Just how lucky I am. I have you and Dillon and such great friends."

Stamos nuzzled her neck. "We have you. Dillon and I are the lucky ones."

Joy turned in his arms and looked up into his moonlit eyes. The dark pools, filled with so much love, humbled her. Framing his strong face in her small hands, she smiled. "You gave me my life back, thank you."

"It'll be a new life, filled with picnics, and diaper changing," he teased, leaning down to kiss her.

As always, Joy melted into him. Her body relaxed against him as she returned his passion. It felt too good to be in his arms.

Taking a step back, she turned serious. "George thinks he can get my name cleared."

Stamos took her hand and led her to the porch swing. They sat together in silence for a while.

"It doesn't matter anymore, Joy."

"Still, it would be nice. I want the world to know that I didn't kill Daisy. I still can't believe Jaime killed her and told Ida that I did it. I still don't understand the whole thing."

Stamos put his comforting arms around her. "According to George, Daisy did plan to fake her death. Your father was to collect the money and they were going to leave the country. Ida learned of the plan and wanted in. I guess Daisy must have told her no. Ida met up with Jaime and fell in love with him."

"I don't remember any mention of Ida back then."

"I know, it's very strange. I almost have the feeling that Ida was really Daisy's daughter. Maybe Daisy figured your father wouldn't marry her if she had a grown daughter. Who knows? George is looking into that angle."

Joy looked at him in surprise. "Wow. So somehow Jaime was sleeping with Ida and Daisy?"

"Yes. I think Ida found out and planned to kill Daisy herself. There is some indication that she might have been the one to plant all the evidence against you. We don't know if Jaime helped her or not, but it looks like he did."

"I guess we'll never know the whole story," Joy commented.

"We might, if Jaime talks."

Joy snuggled against Stamos. "I don't care anymore. They all put me in jail and left me to rot. They are all to blame. I never want to see Jaime again."

"I think it's time to get you to bed." Stamos stood up and offered his hand to Joy.

"Mmm, bed sounds just heavenly." Joy smiled at him giving him what she hoped to be a sexy smile.

"Just bed. You need your sleep."

"Really?" Joy frowned at him and experienced great disappointment when he nodded his head.

*****

Tears poured down her face again. Tomorrow was Thanksgiving and she had every reason to feel grateful. Jaime confessed, but Joy didn't want to know the details, at least not now. She should have been ecstatic, instead she was dying inside.

Stamos hadn't made love to her in over a month. It was inconceivable to her. Feeling stupid, Joy remembered all the new lingerie she bought in the hope of enticing her husband. Stamos would just look mad and stomp away, leaving Joy to feel ashamed.

She had gained weight, but she was pregnant. Gone were the tender smiles, the long looks, and the constant touching. Joy bore it in silence. She didn't want anyone to know that Stamos found her unattractive. It was breaking her heart though. It was being chipped painfully away, day by day.

Oh, she knew that others suspected something was wrong. She could see their wondering looks. It was her problem, she'd suffer it, but it hurt, God it hurt so bad. What had she done? Was she so repulsive?

Stamos came to bed late and rose early. She knew he hoped to avoid her. Joy thought she had known all about loneliness, but this was far worse. It was a torture she wasn't sure she could endure much longer.

Drying her tears, she washed her face. She had a doctor's appointment. She was going alone. That hurt too.

Walking through the kitchen, Joy leaned down, kissed Dillon on his cheek, and gave Bea a weak smile. She hated the pity on Bea's face. She hurried to the truck and took off.

The doctor knew she was upset, but she didn't want to talk about it. He said that everything looked fine. He wanted her to get more rest. He didn't like the circles under her eyes.

Joy stood outside the doctor's office. She didn't want to return home. She couldn't go to Callie's, it would be too humiliating. She had nowhere to go. Her heart sank.

Joy decided to go home. She didn't know very much about relationships, but she needed to end this torture one way or another. It'd become too hard to bear. Getting into the truck, she shook her head. It dawned on her that until her name was cleared, she had no other option but to stay at the ranch.

If Stamos was going to be a mean old hard ass, then she was going to bunk in with the other cowboys. See if that made a difference to mister 'don't come near me' Walker. Two could play at his game.

Joy decided that she needed to confront Stamos right away. Avoiding the house and Bea's pitiful concern, Joy marched to the barn. Benji was hard at work, mucking out the stalls. Stamos was nowhere around.

"Hi, Joy."

"Hey, Benji," Joy greeted with a smile.

"Guess what?"

"Hmmm. I don't know. Why don't you just tell me?"

"Okay." Benji looked around. "Are we alone?"

Joy nodded.

"Stamos got you something. It's out back."

Joy tilted her head and stared at Benji. "Stamos is out back?"

"Yes he's out there with--"

"Benji," Stamos shouted.

Benji gave him a sheepish look. "Sorry, Boss, but--"

"No buts, if you like you can come show Joy what we got her."

"We?" Benji asked, excited.

"Yes, we," Stamos answered smiling, but he was watching Joy the whole time.

Stamos stood before her and took her hand. Joy looked down and snatched it away. Her hurt went too deep to be fixed with a smile.

Stamos frowned, but walked toward the back of the barn without looking back.

Joy stood in place for a minute feeling indecisive. Benji grabbed her hand and pulled. "Come on we have to go see."

Joy followed him to the back of the barn and out the back door. The door opened into one of the many corrals on the property.

Joy saw her present, a beautiful pale Palomino. She was the most beautiful horse Joy had ever seen. She couldn't move. She stared at the horse then at Stamos.

"Do you like it, Joy. Do you?" Benji asked happily.

Joy nodded. "It's the nicest gift I ever received," she told him, her voice quavering.

"We did good, Boss."

"Looks that way," Stamos said softly.

"I can't ride her," Joy told him.

Stamos nodded. "You can after the baby is born."

Joy didn't answer him. She slowly made her way to the mare, her mare. A smile spread across her face as the horse came toward her. Joy put out her hand and the mare put her nose in it, nickering lightly.

Stamos walked to her side and patted the horse's neck. "What are you going to name her?"

"Buttercup."

"No, really."

"Yes, really."

Benji laughed. "It's a girly name isn't it, Boss?"

"You could say that," Stamos replied.

Joy looked up at Stamos. His face looked taut and he frowned. His eyes looked intense. "I can change the name..."

"No, honey," Stamos said, looking into her eyes. He gave her one of his slow sexy grins. "You can call her anything you want."

"Is it time for me to skedaddle?" Benji asked.

Stamos didn't take his eyes off Joy, he just nodded.

Joy took a deep breath. "Is this my consolation prize?"

"What does that mean?"

"Buttercup is supposed to take your place."

Stamos looked confused.

"You're not my best friend anymore. I take it you gave me Buttercup to replace you."

"What in God's name are you talking about? I love you. Of course you're my best friend."

"Nope, sorry bucko, you've been replaced. Maybe Buttercup won't shy away from my touch. Maybe she will listen to my hopes and fears. May she will give the affection I've been miserably lacking this past month. Maybe..."

Stamos drew her into his arms. Joy put up a token fight, then relaxed against him.

"Don't cry, sweetheart. I never meant to hurt you."

"But you did," she sobbed.

Stamos' arms felt comforting as they stroked her back. She wanted to relish in his love, but it was false. She pushed him away. "It's too late." Stamos looked stunned, but she couldn't help it. "You've avoided me like the plague. You made me the fool, dressing up in sexy nightgowns to entice you. I've never been so hurt or ashamed in my life."

"Oh God, Joy. I should have understood. I thought I was doing you a favor by leaving you alone. The doctor told me to let you rest and he said no sex. He didn't tell you?"

Joy shook her head.

"Oh hell. It's been the hardest thing I've had to do. You draw me. I'm a moth to your flame. I had to stay away. You tempted me at every turn and I was afraid I'd lose control."

Joy walked into Stamos' open arms. "You big ox, why didn't you tell me?"

"I thought you knew."

"Well I didn't."

"I know that now."

Joy snuggled against him. "You have a lot of making up to do, you and *The Stamos*."

"I don't think it's a good idea."

"The doctor said I could resume normal activities. Now I know what he meant." Joy melted against him. "I can feel *The Stamos* wanting to make things up."

"You are one crazy woman," Stamos said, as he swung her up into his arms. "I think a whole day of making up is in order. I love you Joy."

Joy smiled at him. "I love you too, now let's get to that making up."

"Yes, Ma'am."

Epilogue

The courtroom was silent, eerily silent as they waited for the judge. Joy looked behind her and smiled at Stamos. He didn't look worried, but she was, immensely so.

It had been a long few months. There was so much paperwork involved and it had her head spinning. Clasping her shaking hands, Joy tried to appear calm. There was so much riding on the judge's decision. He could just as easily refuse to grant her wishes. Worst-case scenario would be that he didn't think she should be out on work release and put her back into jail.

It had been a hard night last night, filled with emotion. There was every chance that she could be taken away without being able to say goodbye. Her heart squeezed tight.

This time she wasn't sure if she could survive prison. She'd changed so much since she'd arrived at the Walker Ranch. She had softened and she had lost her edge. Stamos' love and belief had done it to her. She had enjoyed it, cherished it while it lasted.

Looking back again, she watched Bea and Garrett. Callie was taking care of the children. The children, her heart clenched, would she be able to hold her babies again?

Everyone had thought it was cut and dry and going to court would just be a token requirement until they had gotten word last night from her lawyer that the judge didn't think it was an easy decision. He wanted to examine all the evidence. He wasn't convinced that she was not guilty.

They hadn't slept at all last night. Instead, they made love and held on to each other. Joy got up a few times just to watch the little ones sleep. She had cried and cried. It wasn't fair. She was innocent.

The judge was taking forever. Joy looked back again and spotted George, Harriett, Mable, and Bobby the lawyer, were all sitting, showing support for her. Benji and the rest had wanted to come too, but Stamos insisted that they had too much work to do.

She tried to think positively. She tried to give her problems up to God, but she still had doubt. Few things in her life had ever gone her way and she really expected the worst.

The whole plan had gone haywire. Jamie refused to cooperate or implicate himself in Daisy's murder. Now, Joy wished that she'd just left things alone. She'd done her time or so she thought. Now it was in the judge's hands. Jaime had been convicted of attempted murder and was rotting in prison.

Joy felt so wrung out and her nerves were frayed to the breaking point.

The door opened and they were told to all rise. Her heart began to beat faster and there was a roaring in her ears. All she could do was stare at the judge. Finally, she heard what he was saying. Hearing the words, she slumped against her lawyer.

Stamos was at her side, holding her. "It's good news, baby. We're going home."

Joy looked at him without comprehension. "What?"

"You're free, Joy. We can go home and raise our babies."

"Really?" Joy stood on her own feet and took a deep breath. God had looked down on her today, she knew it in her heart.

Tears filled her eyes as all friends came to hug her one by one. The longest hug was from George, her rock.

"You saved me, George. I wouldn't be here if not for you."

"You deserved to be saved," his voice was gruff. Joy wondered if he was trying not to cry.

Stamos grabbed her hand. "We have a distraught little boy and probably one fussy baby to get to."

The weight of all those years fell from her shoulders. She had been proclaimed innocent. Miracles did happen. Smiling, she allowed Stamos to lead her out of the courthouse.

There, sitting in the car, was Callie and the kids.

"I called her as soon as we got the news. She wanted you to have your children in your arms."

"She's a good friend." Joy let it all sink in.

Dillon was out of the car running to his Ma Ma. Joy scooped him up in a big hug, peppering his face with kisses. Stamos went to the car to get their other bundle of joy.

"She's sleeping like a little angel." Stamos stood next to his wife and son, with his daughter in his arms.

"It all seems a dream," Joy said, gazing at her daughter. She had Joy's lighter brown hair and her eyes were all Stamos. She looked beautiful.

Dillon wanted down. He still had jealousy issues and he didn't like Stamos to hold his sister for very long.

Joy laughed and gathered her daughter. They had thought about many names, but as soon as they hit on Liberty, they knew it had to be. A name representing freedom. It seemed fitting.

Stamos kissed Joy's cheek. "Ready to head home, Mrs. Walker?"

Joy smiled, her heart overflowing. "I'd follow you anywhere, cowboy."

The End

About Kathleen Ball

Kathleen Ball can easily read a book a day. She loves any type of Romance novel, especially Western Romances. Kathleen lives in Fort Worth, Texas with her wonderful husband. She has one son, a Marine. Originally from Rochester, New York, Kathleen finds Texas culture amazing. The more she immerses in it, the more she likes it.

You can find updates on all of Kathleen's novels, releases, and current works in progress at www.kathleenballromance.com.

Made in the USA
San Bernardino, CA
10 October 2016